D0210722

LAST OF THE
OLD GUARD

Books by Louis Auchincloss

Fiction

The Indifferent Children
The Injustice Collectors
Sybil
A Law for the Lion
The Romantic Egoists
The Great World and Timothy Colt
Venus in Sparta
Pursuit of the Prodigal
The House of Five Talents
Portrait in Brownstone
Powers of Attorney
The Rector of Justin
The Embezzler
Tales of Manhattan
A World of Profit
Second Chance
I Come As a Thief
The Partners
The Winthrop Covenant
The Dark Lady
The Country Cousin
The House of the Prophet
The Cat and the King
Watchfires
Narcissa and Other Fables
Exit Lady Masham
The Book Class
Honorable Men
Diary of a Yuppie
Skinny Island
The Golden Calves
Fellow Passengers
The Lady of Situations

False Gods
Three Lives: Tales of Yesteryear
The Collected Stories of Louis Auchincloss
The Education of Oscar Fairfax
The Atonement and Other Stories
The Anniversary and Other Stories
Her Infinite Variety
Manhattan Monologues
The Scarlet Letters
East Side Story
The Young Apollo and Other Stories
The Friend of Women and Other Stories
The Headmaster's Dilemma
Last of the Old Guard

Nonfiction

Reflections of a Jacobite
Pioneers and Caretakers
Motiveless Malignity
Edith Wharton
Richelieu
A Writer's Capital
Reading Henry James
Life, Law and Letters
Persons of Consequence:
Queen Victoria and Her Circle
False Dawn: Women in the
Age of the Sun King
The Vanderbilt Era
Love Without Wings
The Style's the Man
La Gloire: The Roman Empire
of Corneille and Racine
The Man Behind the Book
Theodore Roosevelt
Woodrow Wilson
Writers and Personality

LAST

of the

OLD

GUARD

LOUIS AUCHINCLOSS

HOUGHTON MIFFLIN COMPANY

Boston   New York   2008

For information about permission to reproduce selections from
this book, write to Permissions, Houghton Mifflin Company,
215 Park Avenue South, New York, New York 10003.

www.houghtonmifflinbooks.com

Library of Congress Cataloging-in-Publication Data

Auchincloss, Louis.
Last of the old guard / Louis Auchincloss.
p. cm.
ISBN: 978-0-547-15275-2
1. Lawyers—Fiction. 2. Law firms—Fiction. 3. Practice of law—Fiction.
4. Law partnership—Fiction. 5. Male friendship—Fiction.
6. New York (N.Y.)—Fiction. I. Title.

PS3501.U25L37 2008
813'.54—dc22   2008011291

Book design by Anne Chalmers
Typefaces: Janson Text, Escorial

Printed in the United States of America

DOC 10 9 8 7 6 5 4 3 2 1

TO MY GRANDDAUGHTER,

Lily Sloane Auchincloss

LAST OF THE
OLD GUARD

1

THE DEATH OF MY famous law partner, Ernest Saunders, my lifelong friend and exact contemporary, two years ago, in 1942, at the age of eighty-four, has left me the prey, not only of a peculiar loneliness, the perverse kind that waits on one who is still surrounded by a persistently friendly world, but also the kind that is flooded by the ungovernable tide of mixed reminiscence that inundates the emptiness of old age. Ernest, in his last two years, had tried to distract me from the grief of losing my wife and no longer having enough to do at the office — for, unlike him, I had largely retired — by inducing me to write a history of the firm, and this I had done, as will attest the fat, red, privately printed *Saunders & Suydam*, resting unread in the library of every large New York firm. It is only natural that such histories are consulted only by lawyers checking the index to see if they are mentioned, as it cannot be expected that the author will reveal any failures of his institution or regale the reader with detrimental anecdotes about clients.

It was for this reason of professional tact that I have used in my history only half of the material available to me. There are private memoranda and personal letters in my file no part of which have appeared in my book. Yet they unquestionably contribute to a fuller understanding of the complicated personality of Ernest Saunders. So what to do with them? I finally decided to put them together in this compendium and leave it to my conscientious son, Robert, himself a member of the firm, my "blameless" and faithful Telemachus, "discerning to fulfill this labor," to dispose of as he sees fit. He may well choose to destroy them, in whole or in part.

I share the double name of our great corporate law firm—Saunders & Suydam—which we have never changed, despite our mammoth growth, since he and I founded it in 1883, thus avoiding squabbles among new partners—but my share of the power has been similar to that of the second or third consul in the consulate of Napoleon. Yet Ernest never forgot, for all his reputation as one of the nation's greatest corporation attorneys, that he and I first hung out our shingle as a simple duo with one secretary and that I brought in the first big client.

"It was you who really got us started, Adrian," he constantly reminded me. "And when my tongue was sometimes a bit too acid, it was you who kept people from walking out the door. I may have been feared, but you, old boy, were always loved. And I'm not such an ass as not to know what too many people think makes the world go round."

Ernest wanted my history of the firm to be a monument to the institution he had largely created. He saw it as one of the vital forces that kept the too rapid industrialization of a virgin land within the limits of law. He took a good deal of credit for this. And it was not to dwell on the more personal aspects of this struggle that he wished to dedicate its history. For a fuller comprehension of how it all worked — or at times didn't — one must gain some insight into the personality of Ernest Saunders. Where I wish to speak the whole truth — insofar as it is possible for any man to do so — is to describe my personal reactions to everything about Ernest: my doubts, my enthusiasms, and my changing aspirations in the legal career that I have shared with him. His story and that of myself, Adrian Suydam, are inextricably entwined.

I have had what most people would call a happy and successful life. My sole marriage brought me joy and two children; I have made many good and trusted friends, some in high places; I have accumulated a considerable fortune, and the reputation of my law firm has already been touched on. I have also enjoyed rude health and what I have often been told are striking good looks. But the question remains: Have I made the best use of my unquestioned advantages? Have I even made a respectable use of them?

To say that my family was old New York is to note the principal feature about them. The Suydams had come over with Peter Stuyvesant and never budged farther west than Manhattan Island except to escape the summer heat. They had prospered, like the wiser of their kind, by hanging on to local real estate in the path of the expanding city and had intermarried with the wealthier of the more newly arrived British. I am descended, for example, from Chancellor Livingston as well as peg-leg Peter. By the third quarter of the last century, when I was a boy, the Suydams were among the bulwarks of the rigidly conservative and utterly complacent brownstone society that stretched from Union Square to the East Sixties and thought it had the answer to everything.

They were at first scornful of the new fortunes that inundated their sober streets in the wake of the Civil War. In time they would come to terms with Vanderbilts and Goulds, principally at the altar, but in my youth new money was still odoriferous, and my mother regarded the ball-giving Mrs. Astor as her equal, not because of her empire of squalid tenements but because she had been born a Schermerhorn. Mamma's interior, behind its drab street front, was a Victorian clutter, but as scrupulously brushed and neat as her person, and she presided with sublime composure over a little world where sex existed only in marriage and barely there, and where art was confined to sentimental novels or paintings of lovable pets. She was properly proud of a handsome and well-mannered son, and if she was aware that young men did things of which she could hardly approve, she had no complaint as long as they were kept out of sight. Appearance was all the reality a lady needed. She knew when not to ask questions. She didn't even want to.

Father, I believe, had his doubts, but he did not choose to voice them. Tall, slim, and faultlessly groomed, he made a fine approach when he strolled up Fifth Avenue with his feather-hatted, veiled consort on their way to a Sunday service. He was a great reader of history and spent much time in his dark leathery library through whose closed doors, passing in the hallway, I could sometimes hear the clink of a decanter against a glass. I think that the man Father yearned to have been was the author of *The Conquest of Mexico*. He was kind and gentle with me, his only son, but there was always something restrained in his manner of caring for me, as if he feared that if he intervened too much he might make me too like himself. Did he hope that, left alone, I might turn into something better? Was this love? It was a kind of love, anyway, and I sensibly made the most of it. Did a good instinct tell me that it was all I was going to get from my family in the way of emotional support?

I have said that being of old New York was the most significant thing about my family, but, to me anyway, the most significant thing about my father was that he hadn't fought in the Civil War. Like thousands of his well-to-do contemporaries he had purchased a substitute for $300. This was not at the time considered a base alternative: Father had a wife, a young son, and a goodly amount of real estate to manage. But in the years following the war, when the conflict was romanticized and the glorious victory extolled, a failure to have served became, not a disgrace, but a thing not mentioned on social occasions, like sex or politics. Of course, with children, there was no such inhibition, and at school I sometimes had to suffer the military feats of other boys' fathers being flung in my face. My always-ready fists were a deterrent to any reference to the absence of such feats in my own family, but the comparison was inevitable, and I couldn't vocally resent it. Nor could I bring myself ever to discuss the matter with Father. I was always a sensitive child and knew how deeply it would hurt him. And I loved him. He got all the love that my socially and medically preoccupied mother seemed little to need.

I did, however, discuss the matter with my friend Theodore Roosevelt, whom I called Thee. My parents had a large house on Gramercy Park, and the Roosevelts lived just a block east. Thee was an asthmatic boy, a bit shorter than myself, but he was already opinionated and inclined to be bossy. I knew that his father had not served in the war, and one afternoon in the park I mentioned this to him. To my surprise he turned very red, and I thought for a moment that he was going to punch me.

But he decided to shout at me instead. "My father was too busy helping soldiers to have some of their pay sent directly to their poverty-stricken families to be able to fight! While yours, Suydam, was too busy tearing the last penny out of their families' mortgaged hands to enlist!"

"Oh, go pee in your hat," I retorted in disgust. "I only thought we could talk about it because you and I are in the same boat." I was walking off when I heard him coming up behind me. I whirled around defensively, expecting a blow, but his attitude had changed.

"I'm sorry, Addy. Let's talk." And as we circled the little park together he explained that his mother came from Georgia and had brothers in the Confederate Navy and that his father could not bear the idea of her suffering at having her husband in arms against her own kin. "But my uncles were heroes!" he couldn't help boasting at the end. Thee was all his life to admire fighters, even those on the wrong side.

I privately thought that Thee's father's excuse was thoroughly inadequate, but I could see that the issue was a passionate one to my friend, and I pretended to accept it, as I have pretended to accept quite a few things from the future president, including his rape of the Panama Canal from Colombia. This is undoubtedly one of the reasons that I have maintained my warm friendship with the great Rough Rider throughout our joint lives.

But did my father even have an excuse as frail as that? I fear not. Mother played a role in it, as had Thee's mother, not through her birth but her health. She was actually quite strong and lived into her seventies, but she was a valetudinarian — a fashionable malady in her day — and she made Father feel that he was an indispensable nurse. His weaker nature always bowed to her more obstinate one, and his tragedy was that he was at all times perfectly aware of this.

He was aware indeed of everything. He was content to sit and watch the world go by, providing little but his ironical reflections. If he had hopes for anything or anyone, I think they were for me. I imagine that he liked to think of me as growing up into something he wasn't: strong, blue-eyed, idealistic, with a world before me to conquer and the will to do it with joy. And he hardly dared to touch me for fear that he might blemish the picture. Sometimes I think that I have striven to achieve his ideal as much for his sake as for my own.

It takes all this to explain why Father was the focal point in my life. For much of my childhood he was the only person, with the possible exception of my Irish nurse, Bridey, whom I truly loved. Mother I liked well enough — she was ever kind and gracious when she was not totally self-preoccupied — and my kid sister was, well, a kid sister. On a rare occasion when I socked her I was made to write out a hundred times: "The man who lays a hand upon a woman, save in the way of kindness, is a wretch whom 'twere vile flattery to call a coward."

Understanding Father without ever letting him see how fully I *did* understand him developed, I believe, my character considerably before its normal development, and it may have endowed me with the special vision that I am sure has helped me to such success as I have achieved. For this vision enabled me to perceive at an early age the wide discrepancy between my immediate environment as my parents' social set saw it and as it appeared to me. They saw my father as a leading, active, and proud citizen touchingly attentive to a lovely, sweet, and tragically ailing wife. I saw him as a discontented and often depressed idler at the beck and call of a complaining valetudinarian. But what I very importantly also perceived was that nobody wanted the general view corrected, even those who suspected its validity. It was sanctified by universal acceptance. People liked it that way.

It was thus that I learned to live comfortably with things in which I didn't happen to believe. And really lots of people do that without even thinking about it. I'm sure there are many Christians who don't believe in their hearts in the Virgin Birth. At St. Paul's School I adapted myself easily to the fanatical Christology of the headmaster, and at Harvard I chose friends without regard to the snobbishness of the men of my own background and without in any way criticizing them for their exclusiveness. I learned to take advantage of the total lack of interest of people in ideas you don't express even if they suspect you of harboring them. At Cambridge I was considered a bit of a dude because I dressed so well and kept a horse and buggy, but I was still adequately popular, and even the Cabots and Lowells accepted me.

My social tolerance, never articulated, not only cost me no important friends in my career; it brought me important new ones. Among my New York pals was Jimmy Ulman, the cheerful, high-spirited, attractive, party-loving son of Julius Ulman, the great German-Jewish banker of Wall Street. But Jimmy was the despair of his famous sire, living entirely for pleasure and rarely appearing at the desk assigned him in the paternal institution. Mr. Ulman strongly approved of his son's friendship with me, not only for the opening it provided to the anti-Semitic Knickerbocker society of that day, but because he knew, and knew correctly, that my influence on Jimmy was for the latter's good. What Mr. Ulman did not know was that nobody, even I, was going to turn Jimmy into a banker.

Julius Ulman was a big man in every sense of the word. He was not only a great financier; he had a robust taste for the arts, for good living, for lavish building and entertainment, for the best in food and wine, in horses and carriages. He had a burly and muscular figure, and craggy and powerful features, and he deferred to nobody, summarily brushing aside any racial or religious prejudices that stood in his way. He knew just how to make use of me, but I had an equal knowledge of how to use him.

My parents did not approve of my friendship with Jimmy. Though they rarely voiced any prejudice against Jews, they had no Jewish friends, nor were Jews admitted to any of their clubs. But I knew that the sure way into the paternal heart was any praise of myself, and one Saturday afternoon at a trotting race, strolling with Father on the grounds in an intermission, I propelled him toward the stout figure of the great banker and introduced them before Father quite realized whom he was meeting.

"I am delighted to meet you, Mr. Suydam," Mr. Ulman said heartily. "For it gives me the opportunity to tell you how much I appreciate the fine example that your excellent son provides for my—alas—less excellent one. Your Adrian is everything that a son of your old and distinguished family should be. If my boy could ever become half of what he is, I should be quite content."

After that my father would never hear a word against the Ulmans, and he even prevailed upon my reluctant mother to ask Mr. and Mrs. Ulman for dinner, and they came. I shall have later to describe the vital role that Julius Ulman came to play in my life.

But I must not give the impression that my youth was dissipated, like Jimmy Ulman's, in frivolity. One of the most exciting things that happened to me as a Harvard undergraduate was my being included in Henry Adams's select little course in Anglo-Saxon law. Adams, still under forty, had not yet attained the fame that his histories and memoirs would bring him, but he was well enough known as a brilliant editor and essayist, and, of course, as the descendant of two presidents. His class worked with the early documentation of English court records before the Norman conquest, seeking to substantiate his novel theory that Anglo-Saxon justice owed more to the primitive law of the forest lands of Germany than to any Roman influence. I became so rapt that for a time I was turned rather away from the humdrum joviality of undergraduate pleasures.

I was as fascinated by Adams himself as I was by his

knowledge of ancient law. He stood aside from the world in which we lived and surveyed it without a smirch of the sentimentality in which so many of my contemporaries liked to dip it. Adams would allow no spot on the clear glass through which he dispassionately viewed the universe. And he was charmingly generous with the time he accorded me and showed something like an avuncular interest in my problem of choosing a career.

"Have you an income?" he asked me. Small and balding, he sat back in his low chair touching the tips of his fingers together. "It's a great boon for a young man of any intellect and curiosity not to have to soil his hands in business as it is carried on today. There's not a fortune made since Appomattox that hasn't a stink to it. If your nostrils don't pick it up, it's because you're not close enough."

"What about law?"

"Well, that's better, I suppose, but the big fees come from greasing the wheels of business."

"How about politics, then?"

"Isn't it too late? Commodore Vanderbilt used to boast that he owned the New York legislature, and no doubt he did. The Grant administration took us back to the day of the Neanderthal. The great Ulysses S. was a one-man refutation of the theory of evolution."

"But he won the war!" I insisted stoutly. My secret shame of my father's failure to fight in it had made me something of a militarist.

"And he should have retired on his laurels," Adams retorted.

It was some years before he would publish his great history of the United States in the administrations of Jefferson and Madison, but I was already aware that I was confronting a talent that had more to offer American civilization than the accomplishments of a dozen so-called robber barons. Adams may have been derided by many as a passive non-doer on the national scene, but have those people never heard of the comparative powers of the pen and the sword?

I did not see, however, that the pen would be a resource for me, and on my graduation I entered the law school, as did many of the undecided, on the theory that what one learned there would be useful in almost any career thereafter chosen. And that it has indeed been so in my case is largely attributable to my long partnership with Ernest Saunders, who proved, to me anyway, that a true genius and perfect gentleman could coexist with the Neanderthals of Adams's colorful imagination. It is only fair to add that Adams himself, on whom I called regularly when I was in Washington for the rest of his life, did not agree with me in this.

It was Ernest who most persuaded me to study law. My meeting him as a classmate at Harvard was, as I have already intimated, the most important event in my life. I know it to be a romantic "must" to rate one's beloved wife first in any evaluation of influences exerted on one—but it should nonetheless be obvious to all that my name is known today largely through its association with that of my senior partner. Ernest was a slim, dry, sarcastic, and slightly diminutive youth from New York, the son of a textile factor, who seemed to know everything under the sun without boasting about it. I found myself sitting next to him in an English class early in our sophomore year, and he impressed me as we walked away together afterward with his analysis of *The Scarlet Letter.*

"Art is an obsession," he told me. "That is why it need not relate to anything or anybody but the artist himself. Hawthorne lived completely outside his own time. He hankered for the past, even if it was a cruel and unjust past. He would have been perfectly content to return to a witch-hunting Salem. But all he could do was re-create it in a book. And thus our greatest classic has nothing to do with the contemporary America in which it was written."

"But Hawthorne *did* live in his time," I protested. "He was the friend of a president."

"Franklin Pierce. True. He even wrote a campaign biography of him. And neatly sidestepped the whole issue of slavery."

"Are you implying it's a smart idea to emulate Hawthorne's detachment?"

"Only if you want to write a novel. It so happens I don't. I want my life to *be* a novel. Someone else can write it."

His self-assurance intrigued me. How could this slight and uncolorful fellow see himself in so brave a light? And with my already developing taste for the unusual, I cultivated the society of this lonely, and apparently content to be lonely, young man. I found him even more interesting than I had anticipated. He took absolutely nothing for granted; he seemed devoid of either prejudice or enthusiasm. My social background did not appear in the least to impress him; he accepted my interest in him as the natural desire of a lower intellect to feed on a higher one, yet he betrayed no conceit. It was as if he regarded his mental power as a gift for which he was in no way responsible but for the proper use of which he would be held strictly accountable. He certainly understood that he lacked the money and lineage and background of more socially privileged classmates like myself, about which he could be scathingly sarcastic, but he did not see them as serious obstacles in the path of a determined soul.

When I began to introduce him to my friends, I found that he was accepted more readily than I had anticipated, and I soon made out why. He was different with them than he was with me. He was just as amusing but much less sharp. He never made fun of their amusements and fetishes, or the idleness of much of their lives; he reserved his criticisms to ridicule the things that they too found ridiculous: certain professors, certain politicians, obscure college requirements, fussy family restrictions. Like Falstaff he was not only witty; he created wit in others. However unlike my friends he was, however poor and unathletic, he made them comfortable with themselves.

What eventually I came to understand—and it didn't take me long, for I've never been a fool—was why Ernest treated me so differently than he did my friends. I was his Trojan horse to enter a society to which his background more or less foreclosed him, but a Trojan horse that needed special treatment. I had to be given the better hay of intimacy. He saw that I was smart enough to be amused at his game and even to take some credit for helping him pull it off. It would be tacitly agreed between us never to mention the game. That would have been odious. All this I might have resented had I been a fool, and indeed at first I was a bit hot under the collar. But I pulled myself together and forced myself to realize that it was entirely possible for Ernest to use me and still genuinely to like me. He was not inhuman; he needed at least one person to be a real friend on his upward way. And he never let me down. What had I to lose? Indeed, I had everything to gain. And haven't I?

But there is something else — at least something else to speculate about in a totally private memoir. I have to acknowledge the role that my generally recognized good looks and strong bodily structure have played in my success. Ernest, on the contrary, was an unremarkable figure of a male — presentable, yes, but slight and stooping. It was entirely natural for such a man to envy, to admire, even to be attracted by one so much his physical superior. Oh, I'm not saying that Ernest was homoerotic — he was long married and the father of three — but there's a bit of the female in every man — in varying amounts, of course. All I am suggesting is that my looks may have played some role in the warm and constant friendship that Ernest has been good enough to bestow on me through the years. And in all honesty I must add that I have always been aware of it. And that I may even have taken advantage of it. So in the end, who most used whom? I prefer to bury the issue in the term "symbiosis."

The miracle that I achieved on Ernest's behalf at Harvard can be appreciated only by those who knew the college social life of that day: I got him elected to the Porcellian Club.

A T HARVARD COLLEGE I studied hard, at least in Henry
Adams's class, and at Harvard Law I was adequately
industrious, but I must not give the impression that I was ever
in the least a "greasy grind." Far from it, for in New York and
on Long Island's north shore I led, in the long summers and
multiple weekends, a very active social and sporting life. I became a familiar figure in the cotillions at Gotham balls; I
joined several clubs; I rode in Central Park, and on Long Island I made a name for myself as a master of fox hounds. It
was in this latter field that I renewed my early friendship with
Theodore Roosevelt, which had somewhat lapsed at Harvard
due to my distaste for the rather smelly atmosphere of his
rooms, where he kept so many small specimens of wildlife.
But the fox hunting drew us together again.

This was also the period of my infatuation with Pauline
Lowry. She was the radiantly beautiful only child of a rather
dowdy and elderly couple of old but faded New York vin-
tage who held her forth as the one asset they still had to
keep their place in a society with whose rate of expendi-
ture they could no longer afford to keep up. It was a day
when particular women were publicly acclaimed for their

beauty, even when they were in no other way celebrities. In London, for example, postcards showing striking-looking society women were sometimes sold in stationery stores. Pauline was known in New York well beyond the restricted social circles that she frequented. But she had no vanity about her own beauty. It even seemed to irk her.

"In the past a girl's looks were frequently destroyed by smallpox," she observed. "And that was not always a bad thing. Sometimes it protected her from the wrong man. In Dickens's *Bleak House* it's the true lover who ignores Esther's facial spots."

I was convinced that I was hotly in love with Pauline and was a faithful caller at the Lowrys' modest brownstone on Brooklyn Heights whenever I was in town. But she had many other admirers and showed little preference between them. She did, however, confide in me some of her troubles. She was much concerned about what her parents expected of her.

"They're really counting on me to make what they call a great match. Then they can sing their Nunc Dimittis. It's pathetic, and I hate to let them down. But I can't see my way to doing what they want."

"Would I do for them, do you think?"

"Did you never see a seal swallow a fish? They'd sloop you down! As it is, they're holding their breath."

But Pauline made it clear that she was still bantering. I didn't realize that a young woman's candor did not necessarily indicate a romantic interest. She was a deeply troubled young woman. She trusted me with confidences that most girls would have made only to one of their own sex.

A constant mocker of my infatuation was my dear little Bostonian second cousin, Kate Peyton, the girl who was to become my beloved wife. She was related to me on my father's side: a cousin of his had married into the old, highly respectable, but somewhat reduced in fortune Peytons, who just managed, with the careful planning of their city, to maintain homes on Beacon Street and in Beverly Farms. Kate was a bit on the short side and of only average prettiness, but she more than made up for this with her liveliness, wit, and love of a good time. But nothing escaped her, and her tongue could be sharp indeed. If she was, as Ernest called her when he met her, in her exuberant moments, "a little brown bundle of fun," she was nonetheless as rigidly dutiful and full of high principles as the "hub of the universe" could require. The deep generosity of her frank and honest nature went out to my sister, Violet, the rather pathetic victim of cyclical depressions (she never married), and Kate was frequently our summer visitor in Newport. And, of course, when I was at Harvard Law, I went often to the Peytons' on Beacon Street.

My relations with Kate had always been close. There was a tiresome legend in my family that she had been in love with me since our childhood. She certainly never admitted it, but I will confess that, in the long period when we were "just friends," *I* may have seen our rather distant kinship as a protection from any idea in either of us of a closer tie. This may have been because, though I cherished our friendship, the barbs of her too acute perception sometimes hit sore spots in me. I did not, at least in my callow youth, respond too cheerily to the concept of a mate with such x-ray vision.

Didn't a man have to be something of a hero in his own home? Kate may have freely, even enthusiastically, acknowledged my good points, but she could also harp on what she didn't hesitate to call my worldliness and frivolity.

She had been a boarding schoolmate of Pauline Lowry, whom she much liked, but she thought it prudent to advise me of a peculiarity in the latter's character, not realizing that I already had some notice of it. "You boys have got the poor girl all wrong," she told me. "You're always warbling odes to her beauty. She hates her beauty! She's terrified of being married for it. The way rich girls worry about being married for their money. Yet they always are."

"I don't know that men *marry* for beauty," I retorted. "Though it's certainly the first thing that attracts them."

"Well, it must be nice to have *something* to be married for. I have an old family, but everyone in Boston has that. Often the same one. One can only hope that one has some hidden asset that will attract some man of odd tastes. Frank Latterbury is supposed to have wed a dim and unendowed connection of the Astor family in New York simply for the sake of being able to refer to the queen of your sacred Four Hundred as Cousin Caroline."

"You have wit, dear Kate."

"Oh, men won't marry for that. They hate that in a wife. They only want her, poor thing, to laugh at what they think is theirs."

"The man you marry will be disappointed if he expects that."

But Kate wanted to return to Pauline. "Don't expect too much of her."

"What do you mean by that?"

"Well, for one thing, I don't believe she'll ever marry."

"What makes you say a thing like that?" I demanded, not bothering to hide my agitation.

"It's just a hunch. Everything about her is unlikely. If she were a Catholic and lived in eighteenth-century France she might have retired to one of those elegant convents and spent her life singing Gregorian chants."

Well, Pauline didn't do anything like that, but what she did was strange enough. She put an unbridgeable distance between her social world and herself by eloping with the popular black leader of a fashionable dance orchestra, and settled with him in Paris, where they are said to have been well enough received. I was sorely shocked.

Less so, however, than I would have expected. Perhaps it was that she had lessened her value to me by her choice of mate. I say in my own defense that to marry a black in that benighted day was considered a wild perversity. It may also have been a factor that I was not one of those whose love can actually be swelled by nonrequitement. Still, I was considerably chagrined by the speed of my emotional recovery. Had I really any heart?

As my pursuit of Pauline had been widely observed, I had to put up with the copious sympathy of friends, particularly that of Ernest and Kate, who honestly believed me stricken. Ernest had just won a splendid victory in a moot court trial at law school, and I decided to celebrate this by inviting him and Kate to dine with me at the Ritz.

Over the champagne I would show them that I was no longer forlorn.

Kate picked this up right away, as was made clear by her own exuberance at dinner. There were no barbs that night. I have no doubt that my mother, who, though fond of Kate, thought her no great matrimonial catch, would have attributed her high spirits to the elimination of a rival, but no wedding was on my mind that night. Kate, who in later years would worry that Ernest played too large a role in our life, was all for him then, and wanted to talk about law and what a great team he and I would make. She knew that we were planning to practice together and beamed her approval.

"I look into the future and see the triumph of the great firm of Suydam and Saunders!" she exclaimed. "Or will it be Saunders and Suydam? Perhaps you should change the names around every year. That should keep clients guessing as to who is the real boss. I see Ernest as the ultimate expert on the law, crushing in his logic and research, and Adrian adding the spice of humanity and imagination."

"You make me sound like Portia," I objected.

"And me like Shylock," growled Ernest.

My father, who was always affectionate but almost never intimate with me — or anyone else for that matter — and rarely penetrated beyond a friendly but strictly limited expression of sympathy at any untoward happening in my life, was unexpectedly helpful. Drinking port with me one night after my mother and sister had left the dining room, he offered this unconventional consolation to my supposed misfortune.

"Let me tell you something, Adrian. And you don't have

to say a word in response. I have learned in my life that it is a sacred principle in most people to believe that their feelings of love and grief are a good deal deeper than they actually are. You don't have to be ashamed at the speed with which you may recover from the tender hold that Miss Lowry had over you. You'll be like other men, that's all. Pass the port."

I discussed this with Kate, who, as my graduation approached, was becoming more and more my weekly confidante. Ernest thoroughly approved of our growing intimacy and went so far as to hint that she would be the perfect mate for me. I didn't know what her feelings were for me, as she never flirted, but of course I had to be aware that she was what was then called a *jeune fille à marier*, and had to watch my step. I was determined not to arouse false hopes. But I cherished her friendship; I trusted her good sense, and I always wanted to know what she really thought of me.

"Tell me, Kate," I asked her at last, "do you think I'm fickle?"

"Not really. With Pauline it was partly her beauty and partly your wolfish ambition to grab the most beautiful girl from the rest of the pack. Don't look so hurt. That was only natural. You might say she was your Rosaline, as in *Romeo and Juliet*. But with you, what you're looking for is not going to be the real point. It's what the girls are looking for in you, and you've got it."

"Oh, come off it, Kate. What have I got that other men haven't?"

"Well, maybe it's just that you have a bit more of everything they've got. No, it's more than that." Here she paused, as if in doubt as to the wisdom of continuing, and I realized that we were suddenly no longer bantering but were entering territory where we would be serious. Very serious. "You're an anachronism. You're an aristocrat."

My first reaction was one of disappointment. "Oh, you mean that old Knickerbocker business. But that's all so phony. Those early settlers in Manhattan didn't come out of any European top drawer."

"No. That's not what I mean at all. I mean a real aristocrat. A man who's so sure of what he is that he doesn't feel inferior or superior to any other man. He is what he is, and not in relation to anyone else. You could fight, but only if it's fun to fight. Like a warrior. In the age of chivalry."

"And there aren't any battles for me to fight? Is that what you're getting at when you say I'm an anachronism? Like Don Quixote tilting at windmills?"

"Well, they fight in different ways today. Not always in the way you learned."

"And it's too late for me to learn?"

"That," she exclaimed with something like enthusiasm, "is just what you must find out!"

"But do you think I will?"

"I think you might. But I'm not sure. Or even that I want you to."

I believe that this was the moment when I first realized that I had fallen in love with Kate. Up until then, when thinking of her as a wife, which was inevitable, seeing her as often as I did, I had thought of the emotional backing that this sturdy little woman would offer me in encountering the problems of life. But now it was suddenly different. It was no longer a question of what she could do for me, but of what I could do for her. If she had been right in saying that Pauline had been my Rosaline, she had become my Juliet.

That my parents were aware of the change in me I learned by overhearing my father say to my mother: "I think we may congratulate ourselves, my dear, that Adrian has learned to see more in a woman than beauty."

Mother made no comment. It was obvious that she thought I was throwing myself away, but the utter respectability of the Peytons made the objection otiose.

Kate was above coyness. She accepted my proposal at once, and we agreed to wed sometime before my graduation. But she was less enthusiastic about my plan for a honeymoon that I had thought would tickle her pink. I had suggested that we take a full year off and go around the world.

"But what about the law firm you and Ernest are going to set up?" she wanted to know.

"Oh, Ernest can get that going. Rent the space, buy a law library, and so forth. He'll probably do better without my butting in."

"I don't see that. It should be a joint undertaking."

I'm afraid I was irritated by her failure to respond with more approval to what I had thought was a dazzling idea, and I replied, rather meanly, that considering I was paying for all the initial costs of the firm, the request of a year's delay in joining it was not unreasonable.

"I don't like that argument," she retorted. "And I think I want to talk to Ernest."

I confess that at this point I recalled my old fears about

a spouse with too definite ideas of her own. Were marriage and the law to shut off all my old independence and pleasures?

Ernest, to my surprise and dismay, objected strongly to the protracted honeymoon. He insisted that it was the indulgence of an epicurean side of my nature of which he had always been aware as my danger, but which he had thought had been offset by my hard work at law school. He even threatened to give up the idea of our partnership if I, at its very commencement, was to leave all the organization to him.

Appalled and indignant, I suggested that the three of us meet for dinner at the Ritz, a happy place, to see if we couldn't work the problem out. It proved a most disagreeable meal, at the end of which Kate summed it up as follows:

"Ernest has convinced me that this decision is a fundamental one. He believes, Adrian, that you are facing the crisis of your life. Are you going to resign yourself to the elegant, leisurely life of your family, combining a tepid law practice of family trusts and wills with long vacations in Florida or Newport and extended trips to Europe, or are you going to roll up your sleeves and become a great lawyer?"

I turned to Ernest. "Is that it?"

He nodded pensively. "That old Knickerbocker life has a dangerous charm for you, Adrian. If you give in to it, my alternative will seem hard and sweaty."

"All I want is to see the world first," I protested. "Is that so unreasonable?"

"Yes. Because the world is so fascinating. Circling it will

show you so many other places to visit. You will see some of your old college friends, who will ply you with tempting offers. Fishing in Norway. Hunting tigers in India. Mountain climbing in Switzerland. What do I offer you but the sordid fights of the law?"

I threw down my napkin angrily. "You make it easy for me. I opt for the trip. How about it, Kate?"

Her face was ashen. "You'll be taking it without me," she said.

"Do you mean you're breaking our engagement?"

"It means that *you* are."

My reaction was a violent burst of temper. It seemed to me, in the wildness of that moment, that Kate and Ernest were locked in some kind of sinister conspiracy to reduce my very existence to bondage. I left the restaurant and took a night train to New York. For once I needed my home, my parents.

But I found little support in Father. Once more we shared the after-dinner port, but it was Kate's champion who spoke.

"I have to tell you, my dear boy, that I think your fiancée and your future partner are right. You are indeed at the crossroads. They may exaggerate how critical it is. Of course, you could go around the world and come back and devote yourself fully to the law. But they're right that you'd be flirting with danger. The temptation to lead a slow-paced life is very strong. Look at me. Like me you will have an income sufficient for your clubs, your sports, your Newport summers, a quiet, comfortable, respected, and respectable existence, admired and loved in a restricted but amiable society. With your partner, Saunders, your nights and weekends will for a long time be gone. You will travel, not to the Parthenon or the Taj Mahal, but to attend conferences in the distant offices of foreign clients. But you'll live, my son, as I haven't."

I returned to Cambridge and made up with Kate. We were to be married privately in the near future. I told Ernest that I'd go to work on our new office in New York the first Monday after graduation. My one little piece of regrettable but perhaps understandable male spite was to deny Kate any honeymoon at all. She couldn't have cared less.

KATE AND I WERE MARRIED in my last year at law school, and she lived to celebrate with me our golden anniversary. I cannot say that I have never looked at another woman, or that I have never lusted for one, but I can affirm that I have never been unfaithful or so much as given Kate any just cause for serious jealousy. That any woman with an attractive husband, and particularly one as suspicious as my beloved wife, should have been occasionally unreasonably jealous was inevitable, but I am sure that Kate in her heart always knew that *I* was true.

Her love and support never failed me. She made no secret of the fact that I always came first in her life, and though she was a devoted and caring mother to our two children, I know that there were times when they showed petulance at the contrast between her conjugal and maternal affections. But I do not mean to imply that she was ever subservient to me. Far from it. If I was Jupiter, she was Juno, and a very articulate voice in any decisions I had to make. She was always convinced — and much of the time rightly so — that she provided a needed hand in guiding my destiny, and that, left to my own devices, I might have gone dangerously astray.

In this she always worked hand in glove with Ernest. Their relationship was a strange one, springing as it did entirely from their shared interest in myself. Without that, I do not believe they would have been particularly congenial. Ernest was too cynical and too sarcastic for her stubbornly realistic evaluations, and his ribald jokes did not always jibe with her sober sense of the appropriate, but they both deplored sentimentality and fatuity and insisted on a high performance in any enterprise undertaken, be it work or play. The magnificent garden that she created on our Long Island estate when my prosperity waxed, for example, has attained something like a national celebrity, rivaling that of Ernest's rich abundance of flowers on a neighboring tract.

An example of how sharply Kate could overrule me in a domestic matter can be seen in how she disciplined our son, Bobbie, then ten years old, when he once deliberately disobeyed her, depending on me to shield him from punishment. It was on a lovely spring weekend in the country when boys naturally wish to be outdoors, but Bobbie, whose grades had dropped from sheer laziness, had been told by his mother to stay in the house on Saturday to redo some deficient homework. She was quite right, but I had been planning to join Theodore Roosevelt and one of his boys on a shoreline hike, with the prospect of a lunch on raw clams that we would find. Bobbie immensely admired Uncle Thee, as he called him, and pleaded with me to let him go.

"Mummie wouldn't want me to disappoint Uncle Thee," he insisted.

"Did she say so?" I asked.

"Well, not exactly. But I know she won't mind."

I had my doubts about this, but I gave in to his urgency, and we joined the great man for a vigorous trek through tangled woods and sandy or rocky beaches—"over or under but never around," as Theodore liked to put it. But when we got home I found a Kate facing us whom I would distinctly have preferred to go around. She addressed her son sternly, without so much as acknowledging my presence.

"You disobeyed my direct order, Robert. What excuse do you offer me?"

"Uncle Thee would have been disappointed if I hadn't gone." There was a faint note of defiance in the boy's tone. He would not be the last person to believe that Theodore's name was one to conjure with. But his mother was not impressed.

"You flatter yourself if you think that Mr. Roosevelt would give a passing thought to a naughty boy. And he's certainly not a man to tolerate disobedience to one's mother. You will make up this afternoon for the morning you have wasted. You will not go to the polo match."

Bobbie uttered a little cry of dismay, and even I was taken aback. It was to be a great match, and I was playing. Bobbie loved to watch it of all things.

"Oh, come, Kate, isn't that going a bit far?"

"Are you going to countermand me?" Kate demanded coldly. "If so, you can hire a tutor to discipline your son. I wash my hands of it."

"No, dear. Of course not. No polo match for Bobbie."

Alone with my son I had to endure his bitter protest.

"Why do you always give in to Mummie?" he wanted tearfully to know.

"I only do so when she's right, Bobbie."

"But you always think she's right!"

"You're not apt to be present, my boy, at the times she isn't."

"I don't believe in them!" Bobbie had become shrill. "I want my pop to be the boss! And it's the same way at the office, too. Hopie says Uncle Ernest rules the roost there."

This was a shrewd blow. His sister, Hopeton, was two years older than he and seemed to know everything. I had always regarded her as Pa's darling, and it is hard for a parent to realize how aware children are of one's Achilles' heel. But fortunately I was never so fatuous as to resent the natural nastiness of one's issue.

"And if he does, Bobbie," I answered calmly, "it may be that *he* is always right."

Of course, my debt to Ernest was well known, even to my children. He and I had got off to a fast start as young men when Mr. Ulman threw us a bit of his business, and, being quick to perceive the genius of Ernest, he gave us more and more until the golden moment when Saunders & Suydam, now swollen to a partnership of ten, was appointed general counsel to the whole Ulman bank.

After that it seemed that nothing could stop us, and companies sometimes retained us simply to guarantee that Ernest would not be on the other side. His mind was always fertile with new ideas; he was never impeded by the hurdle of long-established and respected objections. Sitting quietly at the end of a conference table, pale, seemingly detached, black-garbed, always without any papers before him, he would appear to be only half listening to lengthy expositions until he would suddenly nod and murmur, "Have you ever thought of it *this* way?" And then in crisp, clear tones he would enunciate what, in three cases out of four, would be a solution to the problem propounded. It seemed to emanate from within: one rarely saw him in the law library; books were brought to him and he studied them behind closed doors. The only documents on his desk were apt to be those setting forth the arguments of his opponents, and these he glanced through with lightning speed, pouncing like a fox on the weakest points. Then they would be cleared away; appearing an uncluttered self was almost a fetish with him. Arguing before an appellate court, he spoke without notes.

What was I to him? Well, by no means a fifth wheel. I did all the things he didn't do. I took care of the office administration; I was the diplomat who encouraged the promising clerk who was not quite sure of himself and tactfully moderated the one who was too sure, who eased out the men who weren't partner material and reassured those who had been scarred by Ernest's satirical cracks. I saw that the staff was up to snuff and the daily routine smoothly run; I entertained the more important clients and attracted new ones on weekends in country clubs. I presided at the firm's social gatherings and represented the firm at bar association conferences. But I could have been replaced. Ernest could not have been.

We did not become one of the major corporation law firms in the nation until the present century had begun, but in the 1890s we were prosperous and highly reputable, and Ernest and I were still in our middle thirties. And I was already having qualms about the methods some of our clients were using to achieve monopoly in their fields of action. While financial planning in the issuance of stocks and bonds to consummate corporate mergers and reorganizations did not involve us in strikebreaking or price-cutting or kickbacks or the bribing of judges and legislators, one could not be unaware that such things were going on and heartily endorsed by the cheerful and congenial entrepreneurs who consulted us in other matters in our paneled offices on Wall Street.

My reservations intensified one week when I was in Pittsburgh reorganizing a steel company that had been temporarily crippled by a devastating stockholders' suit. I dealt in particular with a bright young vice president who, in order to familiarize me with the whole corporate picture, took me on a tour not only of the company plant but to the part of town where most of the workers lived. In doing the latter he showed himself to be of a more humanitarian frame of mind than the other officers I met.

I needn't here discuss the meanness and desolation of what I saw. The men were largely from middle Europe: Hungarians, Serbs, Ukrainians. Many spoke no English; their homes were soiled and primitive. My guide told me that they were united in nothing but their hatred of their bosses. A recent strike had been bloodily suppressed; scabs had taken many of their jobs. I returned to New York with much to mull over.

Lunching with Ernest at our downtown club, I could talk of nothing but the sordid living conditions of the foreign-born steelworkers. Ernest listened patiently and agreed that it was a pity that nothing was done about it.

"But shouldn't *we* do something?" I wanted to know.

"I don't see what," he answered with a shrug. "Not effectively, anyhow. We're not labor lawyers. Or legislators. Or judges. The remedying of social injustice is hardly our province."

"Yet we represent some of the chief offenders!"

"Not in their offenses. For that they have local or house counsel. There are things they don't choose to discuss with us, and it's not our function to bring them up."

"But surely we could use our influence on them to show a little heart."

"How to lose a client in one easy lesson. Be sensible, my dear Addie. No one's asking for your advice in these matters. The companies we represent seek our expertise in how to handle their corporate infrastructure in the most profitable manner. What we tell them to do or not to do is always strictly within the law. That is all ye know and all ye need to know."

"But you're a man of good will, Ernest. Doesn't all this trouble you a bit?"

"Will its troubling you or me help the poor worker in any way?"

"No, I suppose not."

"You suppose correctly. Then let us dry our idle tears."

"You seem to have yours pretty well under control."

"I hope so. Look, Addie. I'll go a little further. A lot of the agony you see is the birth pain of a new America, the inevitable price of rapid industrial growth. In a single generation we have covered the land with rails, electrified our cities, produced unlimited quantities of gas, steel, coal, and oil. A gigantic force has been loosed, and all we can do is bow to it. And hope that one day a humanitarian force will be developed in reaction, to control it."

"So, in the meanwhile, like ostriches, we can bury our heads in the sand."

"The ostrich is a much-maligned bird. Elizabeth Tudor was the greatest monarch Britain ever had because she solved so many problems by doing nothing about them."

"What about her defeat of the Armada?"

"Oh, a storm took care of that."

I was not convinced. And I really don't know what I would have done had the Spanish War not broken out shortly after this conversation. I had always had a flair for things military, particularly where cavalry was concerned, and I had enthusiastically done my annual service with the National Guard. So it was only to be expected, when my old friend Theodore resigned as assistant secretary of the navy to serve in the war, that I should have traveled to Washington to discuss my joining him. He told me of his plan to organize a cavalry regiment and train it in Texas for battle in Cuba.

"And you're just the kind of volunteer I'm looking for, Adrian," he said heartily, placing a hand on my shoulder. "I know how you ride from our hunting, of course, and I can promise you a commission as a captain at least. We're going to show those decadent Spaniards that men are still men in America. We'll have cowboys from the Wild West and bluebloods from the Knickerbocker Club, and you'll see that it's an unbeatable combination!"

I was certainly fired up. "Of course, I'll have to talk to Kate first. There are the children to consider."

"And do you think I haven't those to consider, too? But don't worry about Kate. She's true blue, like my Edith. She'll know where a man's place is in wartime."

"There's something else as well, Theodore. For you and me especially. I know you don't like to talk about it, but neither of our fathers fought in the great war."

Theodore became very grave at this, and I thought he wasn't going to reply. But after a bit of thought he did. "I won't admit there's anything like a stain to wipe out, but I will admit it's been on my mind. Bless you, my friend. I wish there were more like you, even if you do represent pirates. You won't catch many of *them* shouldering a rifle."

My big surprise was that Theodore proved exactly right about Kate. She did not at all oppose my going to war. She acted as if she had already resigned herself to it as something inevitable. But more than that, she gratifyingly conceded that being a soldier was a part of my nature that she could not and would not oppose.

"I never wanted to be the kind of woman who allows her love to be a bar between her husband and what he deems his duty," she said stoutly. "No matter what she thinks of the duty. No, I want to be a Roman at heart. I like to think I'd even denounce you if you were ever a traitor to the state!"

I smiled. I had never seen her in such a mood. What was she trying to prove? "Well, let's hope it never comes to that!"

"What it means is that I'm trying to be the kind of woman I think you'd be proud of. I knew you were pining to get into this." Kate was very pale now, very determined. I could see that my project was a heavy blow to her and that she was straining every nerve to brace herself to approve it. "I know how strongly you and Theodore espouse Brooks Adams's theory that the fighting male is the hero of the early and finer stages of any great civilization. Later the moneymaker takes over, and that is the start of decadence. Very well. There's still a role for the Adrian Suydams to play before the Ernest Saunderses take over!"

I stared at my wife in astonishment. "Kate! Is *that* what you think of Ernest? Is that what you've always thought?"

"Oh, Ernest is all right. Ernest is what he is. I don't want to get into that. I want you to be Adrian and not Ernest—that's all."

"But it's more than that," I insisted. "You think I'm dominated by Ernest. Is that it?"

"Oh, please, darling, I wish I hadn't mentioned him. I'd rather have you dominated by Theodore if you have to be dominated at all. But you don't! Be Adrian, and I'll be happy."

"Maybe you'd better go with me when I break my news to Ernest. Then you'll see who, if anybody, dominates whom. He's going to be terribly upset."

"Oh, I guess he'll survive. Better, anyway, than I will. I'm going to miss you sadly, my love."

The meeting took place at my downtown club, where the three of us met for lunch. Ernest had already divined my plan, and he had his arguments against it ready.

"Theodore's a cowboy when he's not playing statesman," he pronounced. "If he doesn't have a bear or a wolf to kill, he'll settle for a Spaniard. He and Hearst have raised the rabble against Spain for their own pleasure and profit. Let them fight it out themselves."

"You don't care if the poor Cubans are killed or enslaved?" I demanded sternly. I suppose I wanted Kate to feel my independence.

"It's not my affair, Addie. Nor yours. This empire business is passé, as the European powers will find out soon enough without our interfering."

"You think we have no moral duty to correct flagrant injustices carried out a few miles from our shore?"

Ernest turned to Kate. "Try to put a little sense in him, will you?"

"If Adrian feels he has to go, Ernest, it's not up to me to stop him. There are some things a man must decide for himself. A woman may feel at times that a man's sense of honor is being unduly strained, but she dare not tamper with it. An honor tampered with may be an honor gone. If there's nothing worth dying for, is there anything worth living for?"

"Certainly there is!" Ernest retorted. "There's one's own peace, one's own family, one's own business. Are these things nothing to you, Kate?"

"Certainly not. But I can still see something inspiring in a man's leaving the comfort and security of his home to risk his life liberating a crushed people from the slavery of despots! We need something more in life, Ernest, than the stock market!"

I wanted to put my arms around Kate. I was too moved to say anything. I had not realized how desperately I had been wanting her approval. Now the business of war would be nothing but joy.

Ernest, who smiled at everything, was not smiling now. "I hope, Kate, despite your crack about the market, that you do not deem me so benighted as not to recognize the courage and gallantry of the man who is your husband and my own dearest friend."

"Oh, Ernest, of course not. You see everything. You see too much, that's all. The world needs both you and Adrian. That's something I've understood from the beginning."

Ernest threw up his hands. "All right, Kate. You win. Let him go and be a soldier. I'm sure he'll be a good one and that he'll come back to us safe and sound, with laurels on his brow and medals on his chest. And don't worry about the firm, Addie. I'll mind the shop."

I had to chuckle at this. "That, I assure you, Ernest, is the least of my worries."

Theodore wrote his own history of the Rough Riders in Cuba and their Texan indoctrination, and I have no need or inclination to duplicate his vivid and unforgettable pages. What I am concerned with is the history of my own spiritual development and the evaluation of what Ernest and I have accomplished in our joint lives, as opposed to what we might have.

But I have to set down squarely the fact that I thoroughly enjoyed myself from the moment that I arrived at Theodore's training camp to our return from Cuba after the glorious victory. Of course I was not very seriously tried. There was devastating heat and some bloodshed, yes, but the war was brief and always clearly winnable. Did my joy in it make me a savage? I had a staff job at the front in France in 1918, but I saw enough of the slaughter and filthy trenches to know that any man who enjoyed that had to have a barbarian side to his nature. But in Cuba, with a leader like Theodore to follow in the gallant charge up San Juan Hill, it was still possible, I hope anyway, for a man of good will to get the thrill of a lifetime. There! I've said it. Call me what you will.

I cannot, at any rate, miss the opportunity of giving a small picture of Theodore at his best. He was indisputably a great man, but he was not without faults. He took criticism badly: there were few of his male friends with whom he did not quarrel — sometimes permanently — at one point or another in his lifetime. I have always attributed his splitting his party in the Bull Moose campaign as much to wounded ego as to dislike of Taft. And he might have split with me had I told him so. But I didn't. That was the thing about me. I never lost a friend. But what did I pay for that?

Theodore was always incredible; there is no other word. Out west, in the Badlands, when he and another rancher had captured three horse thieves and were bringing them at gunpoint to justice, they had to hike three days through the wilderness to the nearest sheriff. At night Theodore and his partner took turns at staying awake with a ready rifle to keep an eye on their sleeping prisoners. On Theodore's watch he read *Anna Karenina* by the light of the campfire!

Sharing a tent with him on our march to Santiago, I found him filling in a rare spare moment perusing Henry James's *The Lesson of the Master.*

"What a sniveling ass Harry James is!" he exclaimed in

sudden disgust. "Here in all seriousness he maintains that a young man who aims to become an important novelist shouldn't marry or raise a family to distract him from his work. But wait! Perhaps it was true in his own case. Any sound and sensible wife might have interfered with a husband who spent all his days and nights writing snobbish little tales about Americans who live abroad because they find their own country too vulgar!"

"Well, you must admit, Theodore, that the New York you and I grew up in was hardly a new Athens. As our friend Daisy Chanler used to put it, the so-called Four Hundred would have fled in a body from a poet, a painter, or a clever Frenchman."

"Well, wasn't it a man's duty, then, to stay and make a difference? And anyway, did expatriate Harry have anything to do with the real England he escaped to? The England of Wellington and Nelson and the Charge of the Light Brigade? Heaven forbid! He cuddled up to every fop and dowager in Belgravia!"

I could only reflect silently that in the world in which I chose to live there would always be room for both Theodore and Henry James.

Only a few days later the critic of *The Lesson of the Master* charged up San Juan Hill against a rain of bullets, ensuring for himself and his family the occupation, not only of the governor's mansion in Albany, but of the White House itself.

4

ERNEST, LIKE MYSELF, was already in his early eight-
ies when I was finishing our firm history, but he was
alert to the end of his life, and I have no doubt that he was
fully aware that I was using only a discreetly selected portion
of the material about himself that I had conscientiously assembled. He had never been one to discuss at any length the
idiosyncrasies of his own personality, but he could not but
have suspected that they were the subject of frequent and
critical comment by those who worked with or for him. The
memorandum to me herewith enclosed is the fullest analysis
of his own psyche that, so far as I know, he ever made.

His will named me as his sole executor and cofiduciary
with the Bank of Commerce of his residuary trust for his
family, and also contained a large cash bequest for me in
lieu of statutory commissions, which he knew I wouldn't
take. Because he and I had both been moderate collectors
of art—he eclectically and I limited to American—I used a
part of this legacy to buy a magnificent Martin Heade orchid
in the rich, murky, ominous depths of an Amazonian jungle.
Ernest had said of Heade that he found beauty where it was
most needed and least expected. Was he thinking of the

law on America's rough frontier? The rest of the bequest I gave to Legal Aid, to which the Heade will also go one day. When, as executor, I opened Ernest's safe deposit box, I found, with his personal jewelry and various certificates, this memorandum. Obviously, he knew that my discovery of it would be posthumous.

Memorandum addressed by Ernest Saunders to Adrian Suydam.

It is often said, dear Addie, that we don't know ourselves, and that may well be true, but even so, such theory as we have may be of interest, and I leave you this one.

My parents were second-generation Scottish: my grandfather Saunders and his two brothers had emigrated from Glasgow in the early 1800s to establish a New York City branch of their family's woolen business. My father, Gregory, and his cousins had run the branch with considerable industry and moderate success, and I was reared with my three sisters in a commodious brownstone on Union Square from which Father commuted by foot, regardless of weather, every working day to his office on Gold Street. Though the family remained tightly united and deeply respectful of their Caledonian origin, they had none of the dash or romanticism of Scottish Highlanders. They remained unreconstructed Lowlanders—dour, conservative, and religiously bigoted, who had little interest in any society but their own and that of other similar Scottish émigrés, perfectly content in their strict and unvarying routine of work, prayer, and austere family gatherings. No Saunders would have wasted a minute on the lost cause of the ill-fated Stewarts.

Father dominated our home. He was a large, craggy, formidable man, usually silent except when he spoke for all to hear, gruffly benign to children who behaved themselves according to his precepts and almost terrifying to those who didn't. He had a violent temper and by no means shunned corporal punishment for disobedient offspring. But he was always scrupulously fair; that is, he adhered precisely to his own clearly enunciated principles.

Mother was much softer. She seemed to believe that the harshness of Glaswegian ways was redeemed by domestic love. She had a habit of suddenly hugging or kissing a daughter or a niece when her stern spouse was not present, as if to remind them that they were always subject to a beneficent order that presided unseen over a disciplined and disciplinary world. This did not in the least imply that she harbored any doubts as to the rectitude and rightness of her husband's concept of how matters should be conducted in the more visible scene about us. She was as conservative as any of the family in her sober dress, her muted talk, her sweet sad smiles. But she never lost sight of the golden Jerusalem that awaited the righteous in the end, which would presumably make up for everything else.

I attended a private day school on lower Fifth Avenue, where I got on easily enough with the other boys and brought home high grades. There were no organized athletics, but we played games in the streets and vacant lots, and I soon learned that many of the families of my friends lived in a much more colorful and less ordered fashion than my own. I had for a while a "best" friend, called Danny Herbert, who had lost his mother as a child and been reared by a hard-drinking and flamboyant father wed to a much younger and flirty wife, both of whom Danny frankly detested. He intrigued me by considering his animosity toward his home as a perfectly natural and normal thing. When I quoted the Bible to him, he shrugged and retorted:

"There isn't any reason to honor parents if they're not honorable. It may be true that we have to obey them, but that's only because they're strong and we're still weak. One day that will change. That's our hope, anyway."

"But my mother is always telling me that the real bond is not in strength but in love," I protested. "That the real reason we honor and obey parents is that we love them."

"Do you really love your old man?" Danny had seen my father at his worst, when he had ordered Danny out of our house for using a swear word.

"Yes, of course I do. That's what's expected, isn't it?"

"Expected by *him*, yes. You've just never stopped to think about it. Your father may not be quite as bad as mine, but he's made out of the same material."

I really think, Addie, that this interchange marked the turning point in my life. For a moment I was tempted simply to walk away from the outrageous Danny, but something held me there. There might be a whole new world in what he said. And was I really so stuck on the old one?

These reflections led inevitably to a fatal scene with Mother. One long dull Sunday afternoon I had one of my usual fights with Lila, the sister nearest my age, and she had nastily upset the card table on which I had emptied the envelope of stamps purchased with my allowance for my precious album, sending the stamps all over the room.

I threw the album at her, and she had gone wailing to Mother, who had made me write out a hundred times: "A crumb of bread thrown in jest made Prescott, the historian, blind for life."

Later that night, when it was bedtime, Mother asked me to kiss Lila, to show that all was now well between us.

"But it's not!" I protested, still morose.

"Now, Ernest, don't be like that. I'm sure you're sorry in your heart that you struck her."

"I'm not, and I'd like to do it again. Harder!"

"Ernest! If you go on this way, I'll have to talk to your father. Now sit down and tell Lila that you love her and are sorry for what you did."

"I'm sorry because it's made all this trouble, but I don't love her and never have and never will!"

At this Mother looked very grave indeed. She dismissed the girls to their bedrooms and told me severely to stay.

"Tell me, Ernest, exactly what you meant by that last remark."

"I meant just what I said."

"But in families, we all love each other. There can be no exceptions, at least in families like ours. You love Daddy and me. You must love your sisters, too, perhaps not in quite the same way, but very dearly."

"But I don't love anyone!"

"Ernest, child, what's got into you? You're not going to tell me you don't love me, your own darling, loving mother!"

Oh, the near terror of that moment! I suddenly knew that I had crossed some line and hovered on the verge of a different scene. Perhaps scarily different. I had never seen that expression on Mother's face before. It wasn't affection. Was it terror?

"I don't think I know what love is," I muttered. "I'm not saying I don't like you well enough."

She seized on this. "Maybe what you call 'like' is really love, dear."

"Well, maybe it's what I feel for my friends at school and my sisters—at least some of the time. And Daddy. And Uncle Herbert and Aunt Jo."

"You mean it's all just the same?"

"Yes, more or less. I guess so."

A sensible mother would have let it go at that, but I did not have a sensible mother. She dismissed me to bed, kissing me rather sadly on the forehead, not on the cheek as she usually did. And she spoke to my father that night when he came home from a men's dinner.

Father had only one way to handle a troublesome son. The next day he called me to his study, ordered me to drop my pants, and reddened my backside with a switch.

"That will teach you not to bandy words with your mother," he warned me. "Picking up a lot of crazy notions from your no-good friends on the street!"

I hope I have made it clear that my parents were some-what out of the ordinary. But so was I. Most boys would have passed this off as the kind of thing you had to expect from arbitrary parents and, after a period, ceased to resent it. Not I. I hated my father to the very day of his death.

But I never showed it. That was the big difference. I recognized Father as a force in my life that would be both useless and foolhardy to resist. It would be wiser to use him. He was never a hard man to understand, nor was he such a fool as to demand my love, as my mother so greedily did. What he wanted was my outward loyalty to the things in which he believed; lip service and conventional behavior were all he required. What went on in my brain and soul did not interest him. So long as I was an industrious and respectable Caledonian, shocking nobody and taking my proper place in the community, he was even proud of me. He ultimately wanted me to go into the family business, but he was shrewd enough to see that I might go further in the law, and he managed to send me to Harvard and Harvard Law. Our relations were at all times cool and even cordial.

Mother was different. She *did* care about my private thoughts. A woman wants all of a man, which is why I never fully trusted a woman. I tried to placate Mother by making up the story that I had finally discovered love in my heart—I had no wish for another switching—but I don't think she ever really believed me, and in time I'm afraid her feelings for me became tinged with something resembling dislike. She shuddered at the idea of a world without love, and that was the only world in which I cared to live.

I had learned, anyway, to conduct my own life with my own values, to cultivate my own thoughts and regulate my own ambitions. Other people had to be put up with; some could be used, some ignored, some overcome. But there was never any point in trying to change them; one could only keep them clear of one's inner self. When a man comes to the understanding that no one but himself ever really, *really* cares about him, he has come a long way.

All this, my dear Addie, is to try to explain to you the development of my particular personality. In the Freudian world that has grown up around us, there may very well be other explanations. But I have lived with the conviction that I have a thorough understanding of my own limitations, emotional and intellectual, and my own judgment of just what I can and cannot accomplish in the world is the only true guide that I have had. It has made me very wary of the intrusions of other persons into the territory of my essential self. I came to see that what I might create in life was a perfect law firm. Wasn't that enough? People go on and on about love. Well, that may be right for them. One has only one's own little bag of tricks.

Only two people have entered the formal and plain but well-tended garden of my heart. One was my son, but you know all about him. The other was yourself. I had the wisdom to see at an early date that I was going to need a partner—in far more than just the legal sense—who was equipped with all the qualities I lacked. Perhaps in our long and never failing relationship, on my part anyway, there was an element of the mysterious thing called love.

5

From the end of the Spanish War to my being commissioned a colonel on General Pershing's staff in 1917 was a period of almost two decades during which Ernest and I passed from forty to sixty, and our firm swelled to some seventy lawyers, including twenty partners, and became a power in the land. Of course, most of our progress was owing to the genius of Ernest, but not all. I had my uses too.

Ernest was inclined to be impatient with those who found it difficult to keep up with the rapid pace of his resourceful and highly imaginative mind, and was sometimes overly sharp and biting in his comments to his partners and even to his clients. Many a time I had to make use of my considerable diplomatic talents to keep the peace among members of the firm, and on more than one occasion I had to step in to prevent an important client from actually walking out the door. Only with me was Ernest always malleable, always reasonable. He wholly appreciated the value of our solid alliance and never underestimated the importance of the different ways in which my abilities complemented his. That the firm title was never changed from our two names was not only a good policy for avoiding conflict with ambitious new partners; it well symbolized the basic inner relationship that guided the destinies of the firm.

There were times, particularly after I had achieved a fortune that could have relieved me of gainful labor, when I wondered if I should not do something more directly beneficial to my fellow men, like seeking a position in government, or teaching at a law school, or running a philanthropic organization. But there was always Ernest to dissuade me, and the firm itself, which had become a beloved club as well as a means of employment, and wasn't I already on a number of charitable boards? And then there was the undeniable fact that I had become too comfortable in identifying myself with my big pompous portrait by Lazlo that hung in the great hall of the City Bar Association, showing me, clad in a cutaway and gray vest, seated, or rather enthroned, in a high-backed Italian chair, one hand holding a golden-knobbed cane, authority implicit in the sleek thick graying hair, the lofty noble brow, and the calm, serenely gazing eyes — eyes that anticipated no contradiction. It was the portrait, I liked to think (God help me!), of an American gentleman of the old school who was not ashamed to look like what he was.

Yes, I had allowed myself to believe that the portrait was true. That I really deserved the respect, the near reverence, with which the clerks in the office regarded me, the place on my hostess's right when Kate and I dined out, the prompt invitation from the American ambassador in any European capital that I visited, the applause when I rose on a platform to make the principal address at some public occasion. And I had grown too fond of my wealth, or at least of all the things I could buy with it. In those days our fees were often paid in the stock of new companies, which often multiplied many times in value. I had built a vast red brick, white-columned mansion in Westbury, Long Island, with a brilliant garden that Kate had made famous. There was also, of course, the Beaux Arts residence in Manhattan and a splendid yawl for cruising. My son Bobbie had become a lawyer, and a very good one; he was soon to become a member of my firm. What more could a man ask?

Well, that was the question, wasn't it? Did Kate ever ask it, in the guarded independence of her ever-alert mind? I have never been sure. I have, however, sometimes suspected that she believed I had done as well as she had any right to expect from my capacities, but that it would have been nice had the latter been greater. She was always, of course, the most loyal wife in the world.

What about Ernest and his wife? His attitude toward women has always been both unusual and complex. He did not in the least underestimate their capabilities; he had a clear vision of how subtly the most seemingly docile and obedient wife could achieve dominance over even a forceful and demanding mate. I am not going to get into his estimate of women's abilities in business or the professions, as in his day these had been rarely tested, but I have little doubt that he would have been as unprejudiced there as he was in other fields. He always spotted talent wherever it showed itself. But where he differed from others was in his conviction that women could be very dangerous in their relations with men. I daresay he would not have begrudged them success in activities long monopolized by males, so long as they did not seek to subdue the opposite sex with feminine wiles. Each sex, in his opinion, was better off on its own. The function of marriage was simply to propagate the race.

If Ernest had sexual relations with a woman prior to his marriage to Bessie Barnes, he never, despite our long intimacy, told me of it, and I suspect he hadn't. I doubt that he was even much tempted; his nature was a cool one. But when he chose Bessie for a mate he knew exactly what he was doing. She was plain, sensible, and shrewd. She knew perfectly that she was gaining a spouse who would be faithful, considerate, and very successful in a career that he would always put before anything or anyone else. She faced the fact that she would never be able to influence him to do anything he didn't want to do. And what was more important, and certainly more unusual, was that she recognized in advance that there would be times when she would be deeply disappointed that she did not matter more in his life and wonder if she had made the right decision. That would be the price of marrying a man who did not love her as many women dreamed of being loved. It was a price that she had been willing to pay. Perhaps because she didn't love him as many men dream of being loved.

Anyway, the marriage worked, and indeed it worked better than many more romantically started ones. If they ever had a fight, they kept it strictly in private. Three children were born to them: a son, Mark, and two daughters, Lila Lee and Mary Anne. The girls, unlike their mother, were remarkably pretty, but they would have done better had they inherited some of her brains and staidness. They grew up to love all the usual frivolous things that spoiled and lightheaded young ladies of their day enjoyed: dances, boys, smart clothes, and sentimental novels and plays. Ernest treated them to seemingly good-natured sallies behind which it was not hard to detect a strain of contempt. It was not too hard, anyway, for the girls to detect. Their mother pampered them, a rare weakness in her character. I suspect that she was trying to make up to them for the paternal love that Ernest accorded almost exclusively to his son. A woman of her acuteness could not help but realize that this, at long last, was the first passion of his life. She must have thought it would be futile to oppose it.

Mark was perfect. It was as simple as that. He was not only wonderfully handsome, and romantically so: blond, blue-eyed, muscular, and as lithely coordinated as a panther, he was also kind, generous, idealistic, and infinitely sympathetic. Anyone reading this may well say, "He sounds too good to be true," but that was just what he was.

He was too intelligent and observant not to be fully aware of the emotional cost to his mother and sisters of his father's undisguised preoccupation with him. He loved Ernest deeply, but he also profoundly understood him, and he early saw me as a uniquely valuable ally in the job of curtailing the paternal excesses. I was touched by his confidence and freely professed affection. Almost too much so. I could not help contrasting this golden boy with my good, solid, honest, devoted, but indubitably less brilliant Bobbie, and Bobbie knew this, though I never, of course, expressed it, and even hated myself for thinking it. I had also to cope with Ernest's smoldering jealousy of anyone whom Mark cultivated at what he was too quick to regard as his own cost.

"You're one of the few men Daddy will listen to, Uncle Adrian," Mark told me. It was by the avuncular term that he and his sisters addressed me. "And I wish you'd try to persuade him to take the girls more seriously. They feel he regards them as hopeless dumbbells for whom nothing can be done but marry them off as soon as possible to male dumbbells."

"And how do you suggest that I go about trying to dissuade him?"

"If you could just convince him to stop joking and listen to how they answer a serious question, he might find out that they have a brain, however little use they make of it. If he could only show them that he cared!"

"But does he?"

"That's what Mummie says. But don't you see? You've all given Daddy up. You accept him for what you assume he is. Because he's strong enough to have convinced you that nothing can change him."

"And you think something can?"

"Oh, I think *I* can, Uncle Adrian! Under Daddy's iron front, there's a mine of repressed tenderness."

"Well, if anyone can dig it out, it's you, my boy. In his eyes you can do no wrong. So if anyone can talk to him about your sisters, you should know who it is."

"But wouldn't it be impertinence, coming from a son?"

Well, I had opened up something that *I* should perhaps have let alone. Ernest was very much distressed to hear his beloved son criticize him for the way he treated his daughters. He had somehow convinced himself that Mark held him in the same admiring awe as he held Mark, that each saw the other as beyond reproach, and united, if it came to that, against the whole world. And here was Mark, on the contrary, siding with the perennial opposition!

Ernest did, however, make some effort to be on better terms with Lila Lee and Mary Anne, but his awkwardness only made things worse. His clumsy attempt to feign interest in the activities and amusements of the girls only demonstrated how little interest he really took, and Bessie at last intervened to warn him brusquely to leave them alone. If she never trespassed on his territory, he could do the same with hers.

Ernest did not at this time betray any of his disappointment to his son, and Mark, ever the idealist, and actually encouraged even by such ineffective efforts as his father *had* manifested in following his advice, decided that it was now his duty to induce his sire to make his genius available to more than corporate tycoons. And again he turned to me.

"Daddy likes to complain, Uncle Adrian, that he's written his name on water. Who remembers, he asks, the arguments or briefs of a great lawyer? His works perish, like those of an actor or opera singer. Worse, even, for the latter can now make Victrola records."

"That is true. But isn't your father basically content with his glory in the here and now? He likes to belittle it, yes, but that is only for dramatic effect."

Mark was now a Harvard senior, and Ernest, in 1912, was in his mid-fifties and at the apex of his career. But Mark had always, through me, deeply admired Theodore Roosevelt and felt that the ex-president's career showed how his father's could be widened.

"Daddy should do more for the public as well as himself," he insisted. "I realize that politics is out — that he's too identified with big business. But there's always the Court. He could be a great judge, like Marshall or Holmes. And write beautiful immortal decisions that are works of art in themselves!"

"I don't see him being much like Holmes," I demurred. "Perhaps more like Stephen Field."

"Well, it doesn't matter which. I hardly know one from the other. My point is that he might at last find an outlet for his mighty intellect other than that of making rich clients richer."

I was struck by this. It was perfectly true, of course, that Ernest, for all his vaunted independence, was always in the pay of someone else. It occurred to me that Britain may have profited by having some beautifully educated and economically independent aristocrats to devote their energies and talents to responsible government: like the two Pitts, Peel, Palmerston, Salisbury, even Walpole.

"And what am I supposed to do about this one?" I inquired.

"You know so many of the great, sir. You're a friend of the ex-president. You know Taft. You could talk Daddy up."

"Have you spoken to your father about this?"

"Not yet."

"I suggest you do so. There's no point doing anything behind his back."

After Mark had done this, the three of us had lunch in the Downtown Association, at Ernest's suggestion. The latter was in a restive and petulant mood. He addressed the following remarks to me across the table just as if his son had not been present.

"No matter what we may think we have accomplished in this vale of tears, Addie, we cannot expect to impress our offspring. If I have flattered myself with the idea that I have gained some small reputation at the bar, what is that to Mark? I'm nothing but a doddering old mouthpiece for a handful of moneybags who steal bread from the mouths of poor widows and orphans!"

"Daddy, you know that's not so!" exclaimed his horrified son. "You know that I simply want you to be recognized for the great thinker you are!"

Ernest turned on the young man venomously. "I know you want me to build a reputation on the bench that will act as a smoke screen to cover up a life dedicated to tricking judges and juries into believing that grasping tycoons are really angels in disguise! You want to create an image of Ernest Saunders that will not bring down shame on yourself!"

I realized suddenly the significance of this sickening scene. Ernest was tearing out his own guts as he lashed out sadistically at the son he adored. He saw how deeply he was hurting the beautiful young man and drove himself on with the grim satisfaction of knowing that he was hurting himself even more savagely. Was it his furious disappointment in perceiving that the ability of the boy to judge him so coolly was an indication that the boy's love for him was nothing like what he felt for the boy? Was this very discrepancy a sign that the father's whole life was a farce? Or was it a gleaming suspicion that there might be some truth in his own sardonic evaluation of his legal career?

"Oh, Daddy, don't say these things, please!" I was not the only one at that table to spot the tear in the young man's eye. "You can't mean them. You can't!"

Ernest collapsed. He reached desperately across the table to grab Mark's hand. "Oh, dear boy, dear boy, of course I don't."

I was glad I had taken a private room at the club. After Mark had risen to hug his father, we settled down to a more reasonable discussion of the ways and means of securing a judicial appointment. But I think all three of us recognized that nothing more would be done about it.

And nothing was. But the crack in father-son relations was never quite healed. Mark was more than willing to re-establish peace with his father and to drop all reference to the latter's seeking judicial or administrative positions, but Ernest knew that his son did not regard court victories, no matter how brilliant, as the worthiest application of a talent that should be placed more at the service of his fellow men. To Ernest this was a denigration of his whole legal career, and a denigration from the one person whose approval he wanted more than anything in the world. Mark was more cautious now in giving unsolicited advice to his father, but Ernest sniffed disapproval in the boy's silence, and the old ease in their relationship was sadly altered. Mark rarely left Cambridge now; his weekends home were much curtailed.

Worse, however, much worse, was to follow. Ernest had always been inclined to be critical of his fellow trial lawyers, particularly of those whose pompous oratory in court he liked scathingly to imitate, but his eye for real talent was unerring, nor did he, in recognizing it, exhibit the least jealousy. The lawyer for whom he entertained the greatest admiration was Leonard Straus, a big smooth flashy man who could ingeniously trap a hostile witness into contradicting himself either by the adroit use of a seeming sympathy or by a thunderous assault, as the case required. There were some members of the bar who found him slick and even vulgar, and others who deemed him a great dramatic artist, but he was feared by all but one who opposed him in court.

"Nothing gives me a greater kick than finding Leonard against me in a case," Ernest told me. "When I see that big dark threatening figure, with its gesticulating arm and stout, ringed fist, arise in court, I know we're going to have a glorious battle of wits. I'd almost rather lose to him than win over another. And afterward, whatever the verdict, we always have a hilarious lunch together."

"Can you actually like the guy?"

"I don't know. I never think about that. All I know is that in his company I'm in for a good time."

"But is he straight? There's something about him —"

"I know, I know," Ernest interrupted impatiently. "But there's never been any proof of that. He's been perfectly proper in every case he's had with me."

"Oh, with you, Ernest, of course. He can be sure you'd smell a rat if there was one around."

"A mind as keen and resourceful as Leonard's is always going to see a number of different ways to win a case." Ernest's tone was more reflective now. "And it's certainly true that he hates to lose. One time that I licked him I actually spied tears in his eyes before he pulled himself together with a hearty drink. If he were to perceive there was only one sure path to victory, and that was a shady one, I can't say that I'm a hundred percent sure he wouldn't take it. He wouldn't spurn it right off, anyway."

"I think you've answered my question."

Ernest shrugged, a bit testily. He didn't want to go on with the discussion.

Of course I recalled this interchange when the trial of a state court judge, Ira Lenox, for accepting a bribe from a litigant, broke into the headlines in 1913. There was no real question of the guilt of the defendant who was condemned, but there was in the disbarment proceeding against Leonard Straus for arranging a loan to the justice from a third party, not involved in the trial, which was alleged to be part of the bribe arranged by business associates of the litigant. Straus argued that the loan had been a private matter between him and the judge and was in no way connected with the case before him. He asked Ernest to testify for him as a character witness.

"Of course, you're going to refuse," I told Ernest.

"I'm going to do no such thing," he replied hotly.

"You're going to vouch for that man's good character? Having the doubts you told me you had? Ernest, can you be serious?"

"Nobody's going to ask me anything about my purely inward and irrelevant speculations. I shall simply be asked what was the man's general reputation at the bar. I shall answer truly that it was a good one."

I was about to protest when Ernest, to my astonishment, whirled around and strode out of my office.

I then did something I had never done before. I telegraphed to Mark in Cambridge and asked him to come down to New York and talk to me about his father. He did so, and I explained the situation in my office. He listened gravely and then went to his father's. An hour later both came to mine, and I asked my secretary to close the door and take all my calls. Ernest's face was indeed ominous.

"You have taken it on yourself, Adrian, to interfere in a family matter. Considering our long friendship this may not be entirely unwarranted. But now you're in it, you may as well stay in it. Can you tell me and my son here why it is wrong for me to testify in the Straus case?"

"It's wrong, knowing what you know about the defendant."

"What I know, or what I may have suspected? And suspected without a shred of real evidence? Is it anyone's business but mine what I have dredged up in my idle speculations? Maybe I have fantasized that you're a crook, Adrian. Should that be given any credit or publicity? The question that will be put to me is what Straus's reputation was. Not what my perhaps envious mind consciously or subconsciously thought it should be. And I can honestly and truly answer that before this Lenox case there was hardly a lawyer in town who didn't think Leonard Straus as straight as a lawyer could be!"

"There were two, Daddy," Mark said stoutly. "And those two are in this chamber and the smartest lawyers in town!"

"You needn't try to flatter me, Mark," growled his father. "There are always going to be exceptions to a general rule."

"But where there are two, there are apt to be others."

"You don't *know* that! Even if you tell me that there are plenty of lawyers who think that Straus's good reputation is undeserved, that still doesn't mean he didn't have one."

"But the fact remains, Dad, that you will be helping to acquit a man you suspect is guilty. And doing it voluntarily. For nobody's forcing you to testify."

"You think me dishonorable? Is that it?"

"I think you are contemplating a dishonorable act."

"Adrian!" Ernest cried angrily. "Do you hear that? Tell the boy he's gone crazy!"

"I can't do that, Ernest."

"You agree with him? You?"

"I don't agree with him that it would be dishonorable of you to assert in court that Straus's reputation at the bar was a good one. It was good in the sense that most lawyers assumed it was good."

Ernest turned to his son. "There! Does that satisfy you?"

"It does not. Uncle Adrian is being technical. But like me, he wishes you wouldn't testify."

"That is true, Ernest. Drop the whole thing, I beg of you."

Had Mark not been present, I think he might have done so. But terrible things were going on inside Ernest. It drove him to near madness that his beloved son should question his honor. And how could he remedy it now? If he gave in and declined to testify, wouldn't Mark know that he was simply caving in to his son and his partner, and hadn't really changed his mind? And that a nature fundamentally dishonest had simply been temporarily thwarted?

"It's a pity I don't have the Roman heartlessness of you two." Ernest almost spat the words out. "I have the decadent weakness to want to help a friend in trouble. I shall certainly testify as requested. This meeting is now adjourned. I assume, Mark, that you will take the first train back to Cambridge."

Ernest's testimony did little for his friend, who was disbarred. But it put an end to the happy pride Ernest had always taken in the contemplation of his son's brilliant academic career. Mark, wonderful boy, did everything he could to restore matters to the old footing; he even went so far as to commend his father for his kindness in loaning money to the disbarred Straus to set him up in a new business, but there was a somberness in Ernest's acceptance of his son's repledging of his love that betrayed his lingering soreness and deep hurt.

I think, though, that things might have been returned to the old basis had the full extent of Mark's radicalism not been revealed to his father by his postgraduate plans. It had not occurred to Ernest that Mark might decide against going to law school and decline to take his ultimate place in the great firm that was bound to welcome him.

Of course I knew that Mark had worked enthusiastically on ex-president Roosevelt's Bull Moose campaign and had been rather taken up by the great man to whom I had warmly recommended him. What I did not know was how much more liberal than his hero Mark had waxed in the following two years, becoming the leader of a small group of bright and idealistic Harvard seniors who dedicated themselves to the cause of the underdog and the urging of tighter government controls over those whom TR had been content to call "malefactors of great wealth." I doubt that Ernest was fully aware of this, either, though he certainly knew that his son was not sympathetic with his own firmly Republican Party views. He was, however, inclined to tolerate a certain amount of leftist thinking as the natural product of youth.

"If a man at twenty is a right-winger," he would opine to me, "he's probably a stuffed shirt. Mark is sharpening his teeth, that's all. He'll calm down after a few killings."

But Mark was not only sharpening his teeth; he was planning to use them. He and his group wanted to found a radical journal after graduation to urge their program of political reform, and whose pocket was deep enough to get them started but Mark's? He arrived from Cambridge to consult me about this, coming first to me rather than his father because I was the sole trustee of a half-million-dollar trust that Ernest had set up for him. Under the terms of the indenture only the income was payable to Mark, but the trustee was empowered, in his absolute discretion, to invade the principal for his benefit as well. It was this power, needless to say, that Mark was urging me to exercise over the whole trust. I didn't have to think twice to know what Ernest would say of this.

Mark made a good case for his journal. He quoted from Henry Adams's article on Jay Gould's attempt to corner the gold market in which he prophesied that, unchecked, America's financial giants would one day rule us as despotically as the Russian czars. His knowledge of business practices and constitutional interpretation was impressive and his argument vigorous.

"But the trust was intended for your personal need and protection," I pointed out. "Not to create political revolutions."

"Don't we *all* need to be protected from money pirates?"

"Well, we needn't go into that until we've talked to your father."

"I'm always glad to talk to Dad, but we both know what he's going to say to this."

"Even so, I have a duty to discuss the dissolution of the trust with the man who created it."

Had Ernest known beforehand what it was all about? It was hard to tell with him, but the fixed, rather grim stare on his countenance as Mark talked in the conference between the three of us that followed suggested that he had had a good idea of it. When Mark at last paused, Ernest turned to me.

"And what does the trustee say to all this? After all, it is his responsibility, is it not?"

"It would help him to hear from the creator of the trust what his purpose in setting it up exactly was," I discreetly replied.

"It was for the personal support of the income beneficiary, of course. I set up similar trusts for my daughters."

"But in theirs the trustee was given no power to distribute principal."

"I knew the poor trustee would be constantly harassed by the girls' demands that he exercise such a power. I wanted to spare him that. I thought my son would ask only in a case of genuine need."

Ernest was talking as if Mark were not in the room.

"The need is in the country, Dad," Mark broke in passionately. "And I have identified myself with that need."

"I set up no trust for that" was his father's cold reply. "That trust was for your expenses and nobody else's. If you wish to spend the money for things I have spent my life fighting against, and can persuade your trustee to go along with you, I have nothing more to say. Except that I shall know better in the future how to dispose of my property."

"Oh, Dad," Mark pleaded, "don't be that way!"

"How else can I be, Mark, when I see you calmly embarked on a project to violate a moral trust? I have given you everything you have ever wanted or needed since you were a child, and what do I get in return? A socialistic or even a communistic rag flung in my teeth! How you must despise me!"

"Dad, don't! You're killing me!"

I rose quickly to end the horrid scene. I put my hand on the shoulders of the now bent over and stricken son. "Your father has given you plenty to think over, Mark. Let us postpone all discussion of the trust to another day."

"No, no, you agree with Dad. I see that. You'd never invade the trust." Mark's tone was half sad, half angry. "And I don't want you to now. He calls it a moral trust, and that's what it is. It's really still his money, and I won't touch it.

The journal will just have to wait until I've earned my own dough, though how I'm to do that I don't yet see."

At this Ernest jumped up from the chair behind his desk with a sudden look of hope. "Oh, Mark, would you think now of going to law school? It would prepare you not only for a moneymaking career, but any other you choose. A law degree is never thrown away. And it isn't as if I were asking you to come into my firm or make any commitment to me at all. You'll be free as air, if you'll only apply now to Harvard Law! And we can forget this nasty argument altogether. I didn't really mean a thing I said. I love you, dear boy, and I know you never detested me!"

"Oh, of course I didn't." Mark looked at his father sadly but finally managed a smile. How could you ever change a dad like that, his hopeless shrug seemed to ask.

Mark never went to law school after all, for a pleasanter alternative offered itself, of which even Ernest approved. When he returned to Cambridge it was to discover that he had been awarded a Rhodes scholarship, and his next two years were spent at Oxford, where he immersed himself in sociology, economics, and political history. Ernest, caring now only to be forgiven, crossed the Atlantic some half a dozen times to visit him, and Mark's nature was too generous to hold a grudge, so there was no further observable trouble between them.

The end of the two-year scholarship might have renewed the bad feelings had Mark embarked on some species of radical career, but 1914 brought war instead. Mark did not come home but enlisted in a British officers' training camp, from where he sent this letter:

I hope, Uncle Adrian, that you can be of some help in steering Dad through this crisis. He thinks I've gone mad, and maybe I have, but I have already lost one of the finest friends I ever had fighting in France. People know now this isn't going to be the short war they hoped it would be, and to my mind, considering what the Germans have done in Belgium, civilization itself is at stake. It seems to me that there was a kind of roseate glow over the England of my Oxford years. It's not that I've forgotten my liberal views. I'm well aware that there are two million persons in domestic service in the United Kingdom, which makes it a world quite different from the one I dreamt of it becoming. But the stately homes and stately lives make a pretty picture, and if Britain is doomed to go down, I think I want to go down with her. But we'll take the German barbarians with us, and hope for the future will then lie with a surviving America.

Ernest, as can be imagined, was in a frenzy. He again crossed the now submarine-infested Atlantic to plead vainly with his boy to seek the cancellation of his enlistment on the specious grounds of having no parental consent. He even, unbeknown to Mark, consulted Mr. Page, our ambassador, about ways to annul his commission, and got nowhere. When he returned, his obsession with the war became almost maniacal. Mark might be killed in it; therefore it must be stopped.

"The whole thing is utter madness!" he would exclaim to me. "Both sides are losing the flower of their youth. Europe has been turned over to generals who don't hesitate to slaughter a hundred thousand young men to gain a few yards of mud and barbed wire which they'll lose again in a month's time! Mark has been offered a staff job in Paris because of his perfect French, and wouldn't you think, after his months of combat, he'd have taken it? But no, he turned it down flat! Does he *want* to be killed? He's been twice wounded already!"

There have been moments when I've wondered if there wasn't some truth in Ernest's desperate speculation. Did Mark feel that the beautiful England of his Oxford days had been swept away with the twenty million corpses the war had cost? Was it the country, as I sentimentally conceived it, of Rupert Brooke's poem about the corner of the foreign land that held his body being forever England? Mark seemed the symbol of all we had lost.

The poor young man died in the Battle of Ypres. We feared for some time for Ernest's sanity, but after he had pulled himself together he was never heard to mention his son's name again, and he would raise a silent but arresting hand to anyone who did. It was the only way he could go on with his life.

6

I SHOULD DEVOTE a chapter to some aspects of the practice of law in our rapidly expanding firm. No matter how many new partners we took in, we never changed the firm name, and Ernest always remained the commanding officer, in every sense of the word, and I, despite his insistence that we enjoyed an equal control, was, to use a naval term, actually his "exec." The other partners, all younger, were selected entirely from the much larger body of our associates, or clerks; we never made a member of any lawyer who had not started his practice with us. In that way, Ernest claimed, Saunders & Suydam retained its peculiar individuality and high standards of excellence.

Unlike many of the major downtown law firms in the years before World War II, we had Jewish partners and clerks, but Ernest used a quota to keep them to a distinct minority. We had no blacks because in those days there was no question of blacks in any reputable firm. Ernest justified his quota (a figure that was never publicly acknowledged) by the supposition that after a certain number of Jews was exceeded, the firm would be branded as Jewish and lose a goodly number of clients. But I took issue with him once when he used the quota to oppose a Jew as partner who had converted to Christianity.

"But he's no longer a Jew," I protested.

"You mean religiously," Ernest retorted. "But no one cares about that. The prejudice is entirely racial. No one minds if a man worships Beelzebub so long as he can do the job."

"Well, I look forward to the day when this hateful discrimination is over!"

"Oh, it'll come," Ernest said complacently. "And when it does, all the bigots will claim they were always against prejudice. The liberals will get no credit for the change because everyone will be a liberal."

"Then there's no reward for being a pioneer?"

"There never is. One must wait for the inevitable change."

"Should we have done that in 1861?"

"I think so. Slavery was doomed, anyway. Why kill six hundred thousand young men to hurry up its end? Why was Elizabeth Tudor the author of Britain's greatness? Because she wouldn't fight. She knew the stupid men liked war. She didn't."

"Will that always work?"

"Of course not. But the wise man knows when it will. We'll all be equal one day: blacks, women, Jews. But in the meantime it doesn't pay to rock the boat. Particularly when one has a good seat in it."

Well, I never really went along with this, but I have to admit that Ernest made a very good thing of the interval. Indeed there were very few things of which he intellectually disapproved that he didn't turn to his own advantage. Take the Sherman Antitrust Act, for example. He thought it both ill conceived and ineptly drafted.

"The government has a vague and grumbling hostility to what it calls a monopoly in restraint of trade," he would argue. "Yet it insists that it has no objection to mere size. A corporation, apparently, can be as big as a mountain if it chooses. But bigness, as the public, always sharper than the Congress, perfectly sees, is precisely what leads to monopoly and the squeezing of trade. It is the bigness of Standard Oil that pushes its rivals out of business. The Sherman Act simply obliges companies to split up into smaller units dominated by the same leaders and pass the legal costs of the reorganization on to the public. And meanwhile you and I live very comfortably, thank you very much, on just those legal expenses."

Ernest, of course, had made himself an expert in antitrust litigation. Indeed, he made it a cornerstone of our practice. His creation of the vast Lounsbury Sugar trust, in the very teeth of the act by a brilliant and complicated scheme of holding companies and special stock powers, won the admiration of the New York bar. Clarence Lounsbury, one of the first great American multimillionaires, regarded Ernest as the grand vizier of his sultanate, and consulted him in all matters public and private, and made him a cofiduciary of his domestic trusts.

It was with the Lounsbury family that I noted a new aspect in Ernest's client relations. He came to regard the heirs of the fortune as integral parts of the masterwork he had helped to create. They had to be fitted into his overall plan, trained to preserve what was put in their name and guarded from the rapacious. Any young man or woman who showed signs of seeking a nuptial alliance with a grandchild of the great Clarence was initially viewed by his lawyer and fellow trustee as an unscrupulous fortune hunter.

It was over the marriage of a Lounsbury granddaughter that Ernest and I had a brief falling out. Elena, a lovely girl, had come to my office to ask me to intervene with my partner in his and her grandfather's objection to a penniless but talented young poet whom she wanted to marry. It so happened that I knew the young man, for I kept up with modern letters, and had interviewed him for a grant from a foundation on whose board I sat.

"He's not only a promising poet," I told Ernest. "He struck me as an attractive and thoroughly decent young man."

Ernest showed both surprise and impatience at my intervention. "Are you really standing up for this poetaster, Adrian? What is he after but a pile of gold to support him in his scribbling?"

"Have you read him, may I ask?"

"Do I have to bother? Clarence tells me he's a long-haired pornographic rhymester."

"His hair is as short as yours. And since when have we taken our literary opinions from the likes of Clarence? He would have considered Shakespeare pornographic. If he'd ever read him."

Ernest saw now that I wasn't going to go away. "Well, at least your poet is frank. I'll give him that much. He admitted to me that he has no money and that he can't expect his poems to support him."

"Nor will they. They're caviar to the general. But time may show him to be a good investment. Tell me this, Ernest. Would you ever argue a case in court without first reading your opponent's brief?"

"Of course not. What are you getting at?"

"I'm getting at the fact that for the first time in our long acquaintance you're submitting your judgment to another man's. Are you Clarence's mouthpiece now?"

"Or is he mine?"

"You're dodging the question. Do you take orders from a client?"

These were fighting words. I knew that Ernest held his absolute independence from God or man or any *ism* in the whole wide world as the very essence of his being.

"What's this about, Adrian?" he growled.

"I want you to read the young man's poems yourself."

I walked out of his office with this, but I knew from the way his eyes flashed that I had won. Ernest's evaluation of quality in any field never failed him. Elena's engagement was safe. Her grandfather would be brought around.

7

ERNEST'S ART COLLECTION had no common denominator that I could make out except that each item reflected his infinite curiosity. He had no interest in monetary value, present or future, and he scorned the great tycoon collectors who sought to share, by stamping their names on their accumulations, some of the immortality of the artists whose work they extravagantly purchased. Many great painters, particularly those who did portraits of royalty or despots, made multiple reproductions of their work, either by their own hand (replicas) or by their assistants (copies) or by both, and lawsuits raged over which was which. But Ernest would shrug and say, if you couldn't tell, what did it matter? He was quite willing to argue with a dealer that a portrait that he wanted was a copy and not a replica in order to bring the price down. That it was perfectly painted was enough for him, and his eye was sharp indeed. He once winked at me at a show exhibiting a magnificent Van Gogh that had been sold for a record price to a banker he deemed a fool, and he almost convinced me that it was the work of the painter-doctor at whose sanatorium Van Gogh had stayed.

He had started his collection with old master drawings, and he had some wonderful early sketches by Jacques Louis David.

"David saw men and women as naked animals," he instructed me. "That was the essential to him. Again and again he would first draw a man in the nude and then clothe him. By his clothes," Ernest maintained, "you could tell not only how David viewed him, but how you, a century later, would. Take this clever sketch of the hero Horace defiantly facing the lictors who have come to arrest him for killing his unpatriotic sister. You can see that the warrior is never going to give in, that he's utterly convinced she got what she deserved. And it's clear that David greatly admires Horace's courage and virility. But you can also see the man's a brute."

"You mean the artist sees him so?" I asked. "But wasn't David a terrorist and a regicide? Didn't he do that heartless sketch of Marie Antoinette on her way to the guillotine?"

"Oh, he had no heart. A great painter doesn't need one. He saw both the Horace he admired and the one you despise. On canvas he didn't have to choose between them."

This attitude was further borne out by Ernest's acquisition of a splendid replica of David's famous equestrian portrait of Bonaparte crossing the St. Bernard Pass. It had been a great bargain, for Ernest's agent had half convinced the dealer that it was a copy, though Ernest himself was privately satisfied that the master himself had done most of it.

"You look at that picture, Adrian, and for a time you can't see it as anything but the greatest masterpiece of propaganda for war ever executed. But as you look, you also see that the general depicted wouldn't care if he slaughtered half of Europe, which he almost did. We know that Napoleon actually liked the stink of enemy corpses on the battlefield of victory. Well, can't you almost sniff them in that picture?"

"But David worshiped Napoleon!"

"He also saw him. He was the superrealist. In his great portrait of the chemist Lavoisier and his wife, he stresses many aspects of their beautiful and useful life together. But you can also see, in the very elegance and fine taste of their home and dress, the overprivileged existence that would ultimately bring the chemist and tax farmer to the guillotine. The gloriously handsome naked Romulus in *The Sabine Women* may have the prettiest ass ever painted, but he's also a savage killer."

El Greco did different versions of the same subject, and Ernest possessed an interesting study of the cardinal inquisitor, the great example of which Mrs. Havemeyer had given to the Metropolitan Museum of Art. He loved to point out the sadism in His Eminence's eyes, which would have sent the painter to the stake if recognized. "The Church dictated an artist's subject in those days," Ernest explained. "But many of the great painters were atheists, or at least agnostics, and you can easily supply in many of the sacred pictures that adorn the walls of abbeys and ducal palaces interpretations of biblical stories other than what the Church expected you to. Take, for example, the fresco for which I would happily exchange my entire collection were it available: Piero della Francesca's *Resurrection*."

Here he handed me a color photograph of the masterpiece. An almost massive Christ is emerging from the tomb,

one foot resting solidly on the edge of the open sarcopha-
gus, the other still within, his raised hand holding up a ban-
ner on which a cross is seen. He appears to have paused, as
if to gaze for a moment on the world suddenly reopened
to his sight, though you feel there is nothing before him
that is not known to him. Below him are the four sleeping
soldiers who seem to represent the insignificance of the far-
flung Roman Empire. He takes no note of them, though he
knows they are there, for he knows everything.

"What is happening?" Ernest asked me. "What does it
all mean? All we know is that we are awestruck; we are eerily
apprehensive; we watch with bated breath. The large gray
eyes of the Christ do not appear to take us in; his inexpres-
sive gaze is for the universe and all its mystery. Has he come
to save us, or to punish us, or simply to ignore us? We do
not know the answer, but at least we know there *is* an answer. God help us! If there *be* a God."

"You don't think Piero is trying to tell us that the Christian Church will now take over the world?"

"Something as bad as that? With its religious wars and
massacres of untold thousands over minor disputes of theol-
ogy, with its tortures and burnings, with its suppression of
science and genius? Quite possibly. Whatever it is, it bears
little resemblance to the gentle precepts of the Sermon on
the Mount. Perhaps it is simply the consoling message of
the peace of death that the figure has found in the tomb."

Ernest was never much interested in other people's col-
lections; he used to say that if they were inferior to his own
he was bored, and if superior, he was jealous. He did, however, greatly admire Mrs. Gardner's Venetian palazzo in

Boston, and he had a deep, lifelong respect for J. P. Morgan, as both a man and a collector. He regarded Morgan as a notable exception to the crowd of American business magnates whom his friend Charles Francis Adams, Jr., had dubbed, after a life in railroads, "neither great, nor interesting, nor amusing." I think, too, that Ernest liked the fact that Morgan, differing from the usual multimillionaire, had been born a gentleman and scorned the petty concerns of Mrs. Astor's Four Hundred. He used to tell with approval the story of Morgan's purchase in Turkey of an early Christian treasure consisting of magnificent silver plates depicting the duel of David and Goliath. An unscrupulous rival of Morgan's dealer had tried to discredit the plates by claiming they were modern fakes. Morgan had simply retorted: "Bring me the man who made them, and I'll take everything he's got!"

Morgan fully returned Ernest's admiration; he even tried to persuade him to join his bank as a full partner, but of course Ernest would never leave his firm, and the great organizer of trusts was constrained to content himself with retaining this much-sought-after lawyer on particular occasions, for limited periods.

Ernest played a vital but obscure role in alleviating the Panic of 1907. He sat with other lawyers and bankers all night in Morgan's splendid art-filled library while the host brooded silently over his game of solitaire, listening without comment to each man who came to sit by his desk and in low voice to offer a solution. No one could hear what was being told the solitaire player, but when Ernest had finished, the great man swept his cards aside and rose.

Panic was averted by the well-known brokerage firm of Moore & Schley being saved from insolvency when the hard-to-sell but ultimately valuable shares of Tennessee Coal & Iron, which Moore & Schley had used as security for loans about to be called, were exchanged for immediately salable bonds of U.S. Steel. Was the steel company, in making the exchange, operating patriotically or with a cool view toward future monopoly? Elbridge Gary and Henry Frick argued for the former motive and went down to Washington to persuade President Roosevelt that it was no time to threaten their company with an antitrust suit. They were successful, and the market recovered.

What is not generally known is that Ernest, suspecting correctly that Gary and Frick, with the arrogance of their generation of tycoons, might irritate the president, sent me down to talk with my fellow Rough Rider.

"Well, it's not easy, Addie," Roosevelt told me at a lunch for two served in his office, "to have to deal with men who regard themselves as the political equals of the president of the United States. Mr. Gary seems to think that he and I are like two independent sovereigns working out the terms of an international treaty."

"Of course it's maddening, Thee. I see that. But does their subjective state of mind really have much to do with the result that is achieved? Isn't it only what we agree upon that matters? Napoleon undoubtedly thought he was worth a thousand Thomas Jeffersons, but the Louisiana Purchase still doubled the size of America, and Napoleon lost every acre of the land he had fought to win."

"True, true. You have a point, old boy."

But when in time it became clear that U.S. Steel *had* made a very good deal for itself in warding off a Sherman Act suit, the great TR recalled my intrusion, and though he did not eliminate me as a friend—Rough Riders were sacred to him—there was distinctly a new reserve in his manner with me. I minded this terribly, and brought it up once bitterly with Ernest.

"No good deed goes unpunished," he quipped.

"Where was the good deed?"

"In creating the glory of U.S. Steel."

"Well, I guess I won't get into that. But did *you* know, from the beginning, Ernest, what it was all really about?"

"Do we ever really know what it's all about? We got through the panic, didn't we?"

8

PRIVATE PAPERS left by the dead may present difficult problems for the survivor. Were they left for a
purpose, or was it simply oversight? Should we burn them
unread? Might that not have been the fate of the bulk of
Emily Dickinson's poetry? So read them we must, even if
instructions are left to destroy them. The dead cannot morally bind you not to exercise your discretion. If they want a
paper obliterated they must do it themselves. But let us suppose that we have read the document and find in it material
unfavorable to the writer's reputation. That is my problem
with a series of memoranda written by Ernest Saunders at
different times of his life about aspects of his legal career,
which have come into my possession as his literary executor. I have ducked the question by leaving these papers to
my son. Time may help him to a decision; it can be a great
decider.

The first of these is dated in 1930, when a septuagenar-
ian Ernest was already nostalgically looking back to his early
days of practice. It is titled "A Young Lawyer and Ruth Barnard. Was I a Cad?"

Then there is a penciled note to me. "You never knew
Ruth, did you, Addie?"

And then this text follows:

When I first knew Ruth Barnard, she was a plain girl of stubby stature, with large dark eyes and dark complexion, and, like me, in her late twenties. Something about her seemed to assert that she didn't give a damn about her looks and that you needn't either, as the last thing she was trying to attract was any of the young lawyers who frequented the hospitable house and court of the well-known Tammany judge whose only motherless child she was. Her sharp, occasionally aggressive wit, keen intelligence, and utter lack of shyness made her an effective hostess for her father, and after I had impressed the latter in an oral argument in a case before him and been invited to one of his gatherings, I managed to amuse the two of them and soon became a regular guest.

Judge Barnard's plumage was considerably more colorful than that of his daughter, to whom he was demonstratively devoted. He was a large, cheerful, ebullient man, a famous "character" in New York political circles, a gourmand, a wine bibber, a gambler, and a Tammany adherent in every good and bad sense of the word. It was impossible not to like him, and, so far as I was concerned, unnecessary to judge him. I had no dealings with him in my practice except in open court, and if there were those who saw another side, as you, Addie, would sometimes suggest to me, it was not my business. The people I saw at the Barnard gatherings were certainly very far from the select social group that I met at your and Kate's house, but they included some of the men who ran our city. You and Kate were always trying to hook me up with one of your debutante friends, but I was not at that time looking for a bride.

Which brings me to the question of just what I *was* looking for. Or what, in short, were my needs, emotional or otherwise. The first great lesson of my life had been how to turn my relationship with a harsh and difficult father from a liability into an asset. I read with approval an early entry in the published journals of the young Queen Victoria: "Lord Melbourne here at nine. Discussed my dislike of Mamma." What wisdom! The young sovereign faced up to the fact that one of her duties was to learn to handle the old bitch! She had no room for sentiment, which simply clouds the view. Yet sentiment cannot be wholly eliminated. Without it—or without a proper portion of it—life becomes too dry. My feeling for my son, for example, was excessive: it hurt us both. My affection for you, Addie, was just right: it built a law firm, though you always, I suspect, felt that I used you. But insofar as there was love in my nature—and surely there was some—I loved you.

When one speaks of love, one is never very far from sex. As an adult I don't think I was ever homosexual—the subconscious, of course, may have its tricks—though as a boy I had some pretty heavy "crushes" on handsome members of my own sex. These I confined strictly to my imagination and never even cultivated the friendship of those who aroused them. I saw such urges as nothing but dangerous impediments in any future career; they were like wisdom teeth or appendices, whose only function was to be removed.

Women presented another problem. I do not to this day know if my libido was of an unusual sort, because I have never discussed the matter with another man and certainly never with a woman, except indirectly with the finely intelligent one I eventually married. It has not been my habit to indulge in dangerous confidences that may have a nasty way of being used against you. But I can admit in this paper that I was sometimes upset by violent surges of lust for a particular woman. These always, however, evaporated after a few weeks or months, and were kept under my rigid control, but their very evanescence and the fact that they were apt to be aroused by sluttish women made them bad bases for a marriage. Suddenly, unexpectedly, the beast in the jungle would hold me in his claws, but he would always let me go, and I learned to cope with him, sometimes by as simple an old-time method as a secret visit to a brothel.

Bachelors were not then suspected of being homosexual, and "dates" did not have to end in copulation. I could and did take intelligent girls to a play or a concert without romantic complications, and I had by no means given up the idea of marriage, which was close to a must in a successful legal life. But I was well aware—more so than many naive young men—of the exaggerated romantic expectations of many women, and I had no idea of being stuck with a mate who would want more than I was prepared to offer in the way of physical union. On the other hand, I did not want to be married for the sake of the worldly success that I was quite sure would be mine. My wife would have to be big enough to value me for what I was and care for me for what I was, and I her in the same way. She would not be easy to find, and I was beginning to wonder if Ruth Barnard might not qualify.

She and I had become the best of friends. We both loved the fiction of Henry James and George Meredith; we were passionate enthusiasts of Ibsen's plays and Wagner's operas, and when at her father's gatherings we got into a serious discussion, she became so intent as to ignore the other guests. And when we went out together she insisted on paying half the check, which was almost unheard of in those days, but she made it clear that our relationship was free of any connection with "dating." She made it almost too clear.

"It's not that I disapprove of romance," she told me once. "It's that I don't want it mixed up with the friendship of good talk. We can be like two men together. I want to keep my categories straight, that's all. And, as a matter of fact, if we even *look* romantic to others, it helps me with Dad, as he's dying to get me married, and won't bother me with other guys while you're around. He thinks you're just what the doctor ordered."

"Why? And why is he so anxious to get rid of you? I thought he'd hate to lose you."

"Oh, he would. But he's worried about money. He wants to see me provided for while he's still alive. It's silly because I can always look after myself. But he's stuck with the conventional idea that a lone woman is helpless in the world. Particularly if she's not a beauty or an heiress."

"What does he find so great about me? I'm neither beautiful nor an heir."

"But he thinks you're going places. And he's right, too.

I daresay a palmist could read it in your hand. Don't you feel it yourself, Ernie? I read ambition in your eyes."

"Is that a compliment?"

"No, it's only a statement of fact. I have no objection to ambition, though it's something that seems to have been left out of my makeup. I'm quite content to sit back and view the passing scene."

"But you wouldn't object to ambition in another?"

"What sort of other?"

"Well, in a husband, say."

"Oh, a husband. I don't know anything about husbands."

She then changed the subject, and I had the feeling that she was warning me against what she had previously called a change of categories. But there was no reproach in her tone, and I had the distinct impression that she might not be averse to such a change. I, however, was not ready yet.

But I had to wonder if this woman was not made for me. Did she not know me now almost as well as I knew myself? And I cared no more about her plainness or impecuniousness than she did herself. She had brains and presence and dignity; a husband would never be embarrassed by her. Nor did she have any of what I considered the petty expectations of her sex; she might well be satisfied with a smaller degree of love than other women demanded, particularly if intelligence and congeniality were amply offered instead. I might not be a passionate lover, but I could certainly offer the sexual act, and her own unfamiliarity with it (I took this for granted) might lead her to find my performance adequate. And, truly, might it not be? What did I really know of what other men did?

At our next meeting, in a restaurant before a play, it struck me that Ruth was definitely changing categories, for she asked me personal questions, as if she needed my answers to help her with some problem of her own.

"We have agreed that you are ambitious, Ernie. But I'm not clear as to what will satisfy your ambition. I don't see you as wanting to be a senator or governor, or even a president. Indeed, I don't see you in politics at all. You don't care for riches, except as an incident to something else, and I'm sure you're not interested in writing or teaching. No, you don't care about persuading a public to some proposition of your own. You don't really care about the public, do you?"

"Not a hoot."

"I suppose it must be something about your law firm."

"You're getting warm."

"You adore it!"

I was delighted at her perspicacity. "You've got it. Only a law firm can save a too rapidly expanding America from ruin."

"And you'll be the angel Gabriel?"

"I don't care what name you give me."

"But that would come before anything else?" she demanded. And there was a slight tremor in her tone.

"Oh, yes."

"Even a wife?"

My heart seemed to lose a beat. Did she want to marry me? Was she in love?

"I could answer that with a quote," I replied. "'I could not love thee, Dear, so much, / Loved I not Honour more.'"

"Honor? A law firm? Well, why not? If you feel that way."

"Could you think of being the wife of such a man?"

The waiter appeared with our check, and she seemed relieved as she reached for the coat on the back of her chair.

"Perhaps I'd better wait till he asks me," she said with a smile, and we dropped the subject as we headed for the theater.

Ruth for some time had appeared to be worried about her father. He seemed to be losing his emotional balance. He talked more and in louder tones; his laughs were heavier and more constant, and his jokes, always verging on the crude, now approached the lewd. But he was still the same with me, avuncular if not quasi-paternal. One night, as his guests were leaving, he stayed me with an arm around my shoulders.

"Wait a bit, dear boy. I have something to say to you." He beckoned me to a chair and insisted on fortifying my drink. "No, take this. It may help you to hear what I'm about to tell you." The room was empty now; even Ruth had retired to her room, after warning her father not to keep me up all night.

"Remember, he has to work tomorrow," she told him.

"And do not I?"

The judge now turned to me. "Of course, I have noted the deepening of your friendship with Ruth," he began. "A loving father must note these things. Now don't think I'm going to bring out my shotgun. I don't possess one. Nor am I going to ask you what your intentions are, or even if you have any. When I have finished what I have to say, you may leave the house just as free and uncommitted as when you came in. You will not have to say a word; indeed, I think it might be better if you did not. You will have learned what I want you to learn, and it is this. If you and Ruth see fit to marry, you will not only have my blessing, but the expectation of a considerable inheritance on my demise. My estate may be tangled with debts—I'm being frank with you—but her mother's small fortune is in trust and goes outright to her when I die. Which, considering what my doctor says of my heart, should not be at a very distant date."

"But you look great, sir. I can't believe it."

"You needn't say that, dear fellow. Just say good night."

Which I did, though it was not a good night but a sleepless one. By morning, however, I had decided, with the exuberant relief of a troubled doubt dismissed, to let my future be ruled by this justice of the Appellate Division. I sent a hand-delivered note to tell Ruth that she *had* to dine with me. She did not answer, but she was waiting for me at our customary restaurant at the time I had specified.

But her countenance was somber. "What did you and Daddy talk about last night?" she demanded at once.

"The money I'd get if I marry you," I replied promptly with a grin. "Or should I say the money I'll get *when* I marry you."

"Oh, Ernie, I was afraid of that."

"Why? You were afraid it would put me off? Or on?"

"Oh, I know you don't care about money. You're always going to have it. I mind it being mixed up with the idea of marriage. I mind anything being mixed up with the idea of my marriage but marriage itself. I can't however help it if my situation is different."

"Why is it different? Can't you just marry me?"

The stare that she now accorded me was intense. "You're serious?"

"I was never more so."

"I can't marry you, Ernie."

"You don't love me? You couldn't love me?"

"I didn't say that."

"Then what is it, in God's name?"

"Listen to me, Ernie. And don't interrupt me."

"You have a tale to unfold?"

"Alas, I have."

Indeed, she had. Her father was under serious investigation by the district attorney's office for the acceptance of bribes in no less than six cases, and he had been warned to expect that an indictment would be handed down by the grand jury in a week's time. Furthermore, it seemed only too likely that a conviction would be obtained, and that her father would serve a jail sentence. For two years he had been involved in a disastrous real estate speculation. Ruth ended her sorry tale miserably, hating to have to explain it as her father's desperate effort to render his only child an heiress.

"So you see, Ernie dear, why I can never be your wife."

"Do I see that? I see dark and terrible days ahead for you, but do I see that?"

"Because I will never be the cause of bringing even an ounce of shame—however indirectly—on the law firm that is so sacred to you. Nobody, because of me, will ever be able to say that the senior partner of a great law factory—which yours will surely be—was the son-in-law of a convicted crook!"

"We can talk about that, my dear."

"No! Never, never, never! I swear that by whatever gods there are!"

I soon found that this resolution was not only passionately expressed but passionately kept. Ruth's determination—not to injure me by a marriage that would cast the slightest shadow on my firm—never wavered during her father's trial and sentencing or afterward. I did not argue with her. My silence sufficiently convinced her that I would have renewed my offer had she allowed it.

Did her faith that a loyal Ernest Saunders would still be hers for the asking buoy her indispensably in a time of vicious mental and heartfelt distress? Wouldn't the desertion of the man she was at least beginning to love have been an almost fatal blow? If that be true, the lie in my silence was worth it.

For I would never have married her after her father's conviction. Even though I knew that my firm, any firm, could have easily risen above the minor blot that the crime of one partner's father-in-law might have cast on it, I was never going to risk so much as a minor mud splash on my beloved firm. However hard, however ungallant, that is the way I am and always have been. I offer no apology. A man must love something more than himself.

Ruth had the good luck to lose her father to a heart attack before the prison gates closed on him. Her mother's trust gave her an adequate living, and she ultimately married a brilliant physics professor at Columbia, some twenty years older than herself. It is supposed to have been a happy match. Ruth and I have remained good friends, and she has followed the development of my firm with interest.

9

I HAVE A LETTER from the defendant in the famous do-mestic relations case of *Lounsbury v. Lounsbury*, in which Ernest represented the plaintiff, no part of which have I used in my history of the firm. It was a very ugly litigation and attracted wide notice in the tabloids, but the points of law involved were not important ones, and I felt that the unfavorable light that it shed on Ernest and the courtroom tactics that he employed gave an unfair picture of the attor-ney that he more generally was.

I did not, however, destroy the letter, which was from Mrs. Diana Lounsbury, mother of the children whose cus-tody was legally sought by their grandmother. In the first place, I had solicited the letter myself in my broad search for the true facts of the case; in the second, it illustrated a distinct tendency that I had noted and deplored in the way powerful attorneys in big firms were inclined to act when they felt they had not only the stronger but the morally more ethical (in their opinion) side of a case. It brought out what I sometimes suspected was the latent bully in them.

Ernest was never at his best with women. He tended to think they were underhanded in any combat with the other sex. If true, this might have been attributable to the fact that the struggle was not a fair one, that the male had the advantage of heavier weapons. But Ernest did not take this into account. He used whatever he had, and used it at times roughly. But I'll let Mrs. Lounsbury speak for herself.

Letter from Mrs. Diana Lounsbury to Adrian Suydam, Esq., dated January 6, 1936:
Dear Adrian (as you insist I address you, though "Mister" or "Sir" would be more fitting, given the difference in our ages),

Let me assure you at once that I am only too happy to assist you in your projected history of your firm by supplying this personal account of the famous case of *Lounsbury v. Lounsbury*. If it was your partner, Mr. Saunders, who made such hash of my life, it was nonetheless you who helped me put it back together, and at the expense, too, of your pain at appearing at odds with the firm that has been the love of your life, even though it has been the scourge of mine.

If I am going to tell the whole story of what your partner did to me, I must be fair and tell the whole story of what I did to him, or to his favorite client. You are familiar with a good deal of it, but by no means all. You know, of course, that I and my sister, Elena, were brought up in Paris, as the children of expatriate parents, and that in the early 1920s we were roughly the same age as the century. We were also, if I say so myself, not only young but beautiful and merry of heart, determined, like so many of our contemporaries, to make up in revelry for the gloom of the war years. The generation of Americans who shared our youth in the City of Light had not yet been dubbed a lost one.

Our mother, Deborah Lyons, must bear some responsibility for what we became. Our father, a charming idler, exempted from serious work by the tuberculosis that slew him at age thirty, had settled in France because his slender income went further there than in his native New York. After his death, Mother remained. She had woven a comfortable nest for herself on the fringes of a glittering international set and had been clever enough to glean more economic assistance from it than fringe dwellers usually do.

How did she do it? One may well ask, for unlike her daughters she was large and bony and plain, with craggy features, dressed usually in simple black, with black hair pulled straight back and tied in a knot. Yet she quite wonderfully gave the impression of a woman of sound common sense and salty realism who was not in the least dazzled by rank or wealth, whose friendship was deeply sincere and whose shrewd knowledge of the great world made her advice eagerly sought by naughty wives and straying husbands. She had indeed made herself a kind of oracle in the society that she cherished, and was supposed to have a heart of gold. It came as the shock of my life when, secretly supported by the infinite resources of my mother-in-law, she appeared in court as a witness against me. I had ceased, of course, by then to be an asset to her.

Mother had buried deep from the eyes of the world and from her daughters a profound snobbishness. She collected friends with the avidity of a J. P. Morgan seeking art treasures: royalty in exile and South American millionaires, Eastern princes and maharajahs, English peers and movie stars. And she always had a much-touted humane reason for each new acquisition: her heart bled for a Russian grand duchess whose husband had been shot by the reds; she had discovered a well of hidden wit in a supposed numbskull of a monarch; she pitied the basic insecurity of a peculiarly vulgar tycoon who, she claimed, was a secret philanthropist. I sometimes wonder now if she ever really loved anyone. Perhaps my handsome father, who married her despite her poverty and plainness. Or is that just my stubborn romanticism?

Mother, at any rate, demonstrated a lively affection for Elena and myself, and indeed we were good props to her act as the poor but devoted widowed mother of two lovely if unendowed girls. She of course wanted us to marry well, and she gave us total freedom of action while warning us that, though almost everything was tolerated in her set, it was at the price of not throwing things in people's faces. Elena and I took distinct advantage of our liberty. It was not then generally accepted for unwed girls to have affairs, but exceptions were made, and in our Paris and Riviera, sleeping with an Austrian archduke was not the same thing as sleeping with a penniless man with no handle to his name. My sister and I certainly did not preserve our virginity, but neither were we what is vulgarly known as "easy lays." The bad publicity to which we were later exposed was spitefully exaggerated.

The first sign of trouble in my carefree way of life came during my affair with Camor Howdie, son and heir of the Maharajah of Panja. Camor was a graduate of Eton and

Oxford; he was flawlessly educated and divinely handsome, and I was crazy about him. And crazy, too, for I actually hoped to marry him. Mother harbored no racial or religious prejudice; she regarded any such inhibitions simply as tools to use against ineligible beaux of her daughters who might be subject to them. She saw me complacently as a dazzling maharanee covered with diamonds. But a rapid disillusionment awaited us.

"Marriage?" a startled Camor exclaimed when I first mentioned the word to him. "My dear Diana, what on earth can you be thinking of?"

"Why, just that."

"You mean with me?"

"Who else?"

"Have you taken leave of your senses? Don't you know that I have to marry an Indian girl? Several candidates have already been selected."

"But American girls are all the rage today!" I protested. "You'll find those Oriental prejudices not hard to overcome."

"But even if that were so, my bride would have to be pure as can be. The good citizens of Panja are not accustomed to picking their maharanees from the golden beaches of the Riviera."

I gave vent to a real expression of anger. "Are you calling me a whore?"

"Don't be ridiculous. You know as well as I do what it's all about. Let us consider the subject closed."

Nor would he ever reopen it with me. I put an end to the affair and discovered to my surprise that my heart was not broken. But the world was different. I now understood that a poor girl without a noble name who expects to marry had better learn to watch her step. Only the rich or well-born could dispense with virtue.

The second and even deadlier blow came with Elena's divorce. She had married an English beer baron, almost old enough to be her father, but a ruddy vigorous man who desired her lustily and was of a jealous and possessive temperament. I assumed that satisfying the lecherous urgings of such an ape would not be too great a price for enjoying his millions—that a woman of Elena's capacities might even like it—but I was sadly mistaken. Elena soon began to find herself disgusted by her mate, and the violence of her reaction plunged her into an indiscreet affair with an attractive London man about town, which resulted in her being caught in flagrante delicto by the baron's detectives. In the scandalous and widely publicized suit that followed, Elena ended up not only divorced but penniless, and she returned to Mother and me in Paris, accompanied by a reputation that did us all little good.

It was then that Russell Lounsbury began to appear to me as a possible means of salvation. He was a stout and dignified bachelor of sixty-odd, grave of demeanor, well mannered and smartly clad, the idle only son of the late Clarence, sugar tycoon, and of his octogenarian widow, who occupied a vast Tudor structure on Fifth Avenue and an even vaster one, though in French Renaissance style, in Newport. He had four married sisters, but he was the sole male Lounsbury, and it helped his disinclination to either marry or go into the family business to spend much of the year in Paris, away from the clamoring maternal and sibling urgings that he take both these steps. He had rented a fine old *hôtel* in the Faubourg St. Germain, collected academic paintings by Bouguereau, Gérôme, and Alma-Tadema, and was received by the *gratin* of the old nobility. But he drank—quietly and usually unobtrusively. Still, he drank.

He liked Mother and was a frequent caller at our flat. She may even have once had the idea of wedding him, but soon saw there was little hope of overcoming his aversion to the altar, even with the assurance of a *mariage blanc*. She had to content herself with the occasional gift of a work of art that she could secretly sell, but she could never persuade him to venture into postimpressionist art, then such a bargain. She did not fail, however, to note that he seemed to have a different eye for me than he did for women in general, even when they were young and well favored.

"I always rather assumed Russell was a fag," she mused to me one day. "A repressed one, perhaps, but still a fag. Now I'm beginning to wonder. The way he looks at you, my dear! Maybe he's the answer to a maiden's prayer. But do go slowly, Diana. The fortune's immense."

"You mean I'd better be more maidenly?"

"Well, it never hurts, you know."

Apparently I was maidenly enough, for dear old Russell, after taking me to two interminable performances of Corneille at the Comédie-Française, actually proposed to me, gravely and without having made a single pass. He seemed almost to be apologizing for offering me the haven from destitution that he knew I couldn't refuse. It was as if he were ashamed of taking unfair advantage of me.

Of course, I accepted him. Mother would have kicked me out of the flat if I hadn't. We were married in Paris, and it was all a good deal easier than I had expected. Russell treated me as if I were the prize piece of his art collection; he was almost painfully polite and careful not to interfere with my daily habits and routine. His lovemaking was furtive and clumsy, but it was also rare, as he seemed not to wish to bother me too often with something in which I obviously took little pleasure, so I hardly minded it. He bought me anything I wanted and took ample care of Mother and Elena. Indeed, I had to restrain him from satisfying all the former's demands; it was shocking how freely she plunged a greedy hand into his pocket. Yes, I must say, his conduct was exemplary. He even tried, without too much success, to cut down on his drinking.

I had prepared myself for the shock of his family's disapproval of our marriage, but I found, to my astonishment, when he took me to New York to meet the family, that I was greeted with open arms. This suggested that his mother and sisters had had grave conferences before deciding upon this obviously united action. I have since made out that they must have dreaded that he would face them with something much worse and were relieved to recognize that I came from respectable American forebears and was young enough to produce a male Lounsbury child. If some of the derogatory anecdotes that clustered about myself and my immediate family had come to their ears, it was all in conveniently distant France, and Russell and I had agreed to spend at least our winters in New York, to be near his old mother in what would presumably be her last years.

My knowledge of my own mother should have alerted me to the fact that a female parent can be two very different persons at the same time. I had no conception then that Mrs. Lounsbury was anything but a kindly if close-minded old dowager, understandably proud of her unimpeachable social position and totally satisfied with being an adored mother and grandmother and the benevolent mistress of the many in her employ. She was small and dumpy but carried herself with a rather regal dignity. She had to reach up when she clasped a fabulous diamond necklace around my neck, murmuring: "My dear husband told me to save this for Russell's wife if he should ever marry. And now, thank the good Lord, he has."

Gratified by this reception, I settled myself quite comfortably in the big house in the East Seventies that Russell took for us and for a time rather enjoyed lavishly entertaining a host of new friends and relations. It was certainly not a more entertaining group of my Paris crowd, but everyone was friendly, and all were not dull, and I enjoyed spending oodles of money on myself. Best of all were the annual spring trips to France. Everything, it was true, was interrupted by a painful pregnancy, unexpected in view of the briefness and rarity of our sexual relations, but the birth of twin boys greatly enhanced my position in the family. Like a wife in old China I was conscious of a tightening of the respect in which I was held.

If Russell was happy in our marriage—which was hard to tell in a man so undemonstrative—it was certainly not evidenced by his drinking, which grew steadily worse. I learned to watch him at parties, and would take him home at the first sign of his thickening speech. He was always quietly submissive, and after a time I got into the habit of returning to the abandoned festivities. Eventually I simply put him in the limo, and the chauffeur would take him home. And finally came the time when he wouldn't go out at all, and people invited me without him. I did not disturb him when I came home, for, after his humble and painful admittance of a sudden impotence, we had agreed on separate bedrooms. I could not be expected to mind this.

Betty Shallcross, the most direct and outspoken of his four highly competent and self-assured sisters, and the one I found the most sympathetic, advised me frankly that the family thought I was not taking adequate steps to control his drinking.

"I'm not taking any," I admitted freely. "What can I do? Put him in an asylum? I'd have to commit him, and how can I do that? He's perfectly sane."

"We feel that you have more influence on him than perhaps you know. Certainly more than you seem to be using. The way he's going on will kill him. And it's to your interest, Diana, to keep him with us." Betty now put a new emphasis into her tone. "To your *personal* interest, my dear. In more ways than one."

I stared at her. "In more ways than my need for a loving spouse?" I asked, with a touch of sarcasm.

"Well, do you happen to know how my father set us all up? I mean, financially?"

"No. Russell has never discussed money with me."

"And now I'll tell you why. Daddy had a phobia about what he called grasping in-laws and was determined to keep every penny he had in the blood. Everything he left is in iron-bound trust for Mummie and the children. On death it goes to their issue or the issue of the others. Not a cent to a spouse. When Russell dies his trust will go to your boys."

"But Russell must have something besides his trust!" I protested uneasily.

"It can't be much after the way you and he've been living. You'd have to get an allowance for your personal expenses from the surrogate out of your boys' money. And that would stop when they come of age."

When I did take steps—unsuccessful ones—to reduce Russell's drinking, it was later held against me by my detractors. It was said that I had let him drink all he wanted when I believed I would profit by his demise and only tried to stop him when I learned that I wouldn't. But I have become hardened to slander.

As Russell sank more and more into drink, he grew increasingly remote and spent much of his days at his club, between the bar and the room where he played backgammon. He was always politely considerate with me—rather ceremoniously so—but he lived in a different world now, and did not even pay much attention to our little boys. Nor, I am afraid, did I. I have never been overfond of small children—one is of course amused when they are cute—but mine, although they are well-enough-looking lads today—were not lovely tots. They were not identical twins. Philip was something of a lout and Tony a near dwarf, and they doted on their nanny, who took complete possession of them. Indeed nothing in our big and pompous house seemed to need my attention: a lofty English butler adroitly and quietly handled a well-trained staff. Russell had learned early how to make people work for him.

I could no longer persuade my husband, in his growing inertia, to cross the Atlantic, but he urged me to go without him, and after a brief protest I did so, at first only for a month's stay but soon for longer periods. Mother and Elena were now beautifully set up in a fine flat in the Parc Monceau, and I was welcomed back by all my old crowd. I must admit we cut quite a wraith through the town.

But I didn't—I promise you, Adrian, and why should I lie to you?—have an affair so long as Russell lived. It was after his death from a stroke that I began to lose my balance. There suddenly seemed very little point in my life. Though I found myself as poor as my sister-in-law had predicted, my mother-in-law generously (at least so I then supposed) paid me an adequate allowance and did not object to my spending so much time abroad. She even suggested, and I foolishly agreed, that the boys move into her vast abode, where she could keep a closer eye on them and where there would be a suite always available for what she hoped would be my frequent visits. This seemed satisfactory to all concerned. I crossed the ocean four times a year, always in a first-class cabin aboard a luxury liner, and thought I was having my cake and eating it too.

Well, you've read about Paris in the Roaring Twenties. It was a giddy place, and—oh, I face it!—I was a giddy girl. Not nearly as giddy as was later claimed, but giddy enough. I did have affairs with the Grand Duke Peter and

Lord Lancaster Ames. And as for Sophie Laplace, well, yes, there was one night when, drunk with champagne, I passed out and came to in the bed and in the arms of that notorious lesbian. Your partner learned it from his Sherlock Holmes of a detective.

At last came the fatal day when my allowance was suddenly stopped. My appeals went unanswered, and I was obliged to cross the Atlantic to face my uncommunicative mother-in-law. I was denied admission when I rang her doorbell, nor would a relentless butler allow me to see my sons. I took a suite at the Plaza on wobbly credit, and it was there that you called on me.

Oh, Adrian, you gave me hope! You explained that Mrs. Lounsbury was your partner Ernest Saunders's personal client, but that as domestic relations was a department of yours in the firm, he wanted you to open negotiations with me and see if this matter could not be settled out of court. Oh, you were very kind! I remember your exact words.

"I am afraid, Mrs. Lounsbury, that reported versions of your life abroad have given rise to a conviction in your mother-in-law that you are, at least temporarily, not a proper person to have custody of your boys. I do not myself have any reason to believe that is so. But it is my duty to warn you that your activities have been subject to a very close professional scrutiny, not at all at my instigation, but which may confront you with some embarrassing witnesses at a trial. Of course, you must at once retain your own counsel, but meanwhile I can tell you the terms on which your mother-in-law will settle."

"Go ahead," I told you, breathless with apprehension.

You then explained that if I would surrender legal custody of my boys to their grandmother, my allowance would be continued for my lifetime. I would also be given rights of visitation to the children on specified holidays and have them for a month in the summer, in a cottage on their grandmother's estate in Newport.

"And on the old lady's death?" I demanded.

"Custody would pass to one of her daughters."

Well, angry as I was, I could see that this, under the circumstances, was not really so bad a deal. That month in the summer might be enough to maintain the boys' affection, or whatever was left of it, and when their old beast of a grandmother at last kicked the bucket, I could probably count on Betty Shallcross to be decent to me. Betty had had her own little adventures. I got a lawyer and he agreed with me, when he heard that I had been watched. I accepted.

But the agreement failed. Saunders was outraged. He maintained that you had exceeded your instructions in offering me such wide visitation rights. I see now that you probably had. Your kind heart had revolted against the original terms, and you had hoped that, armed with my acceptance, my enemies would soften their demands. But my mother-in-law had insisted that the visitation rights should be entirely subject to her discretion and would depend on how far I had come in reforming my "promiscuous way of life." Also that the allowance should cease on my remarriage or "living in sin" with a man.

I knew that I could not live with myself if I ate this dirt, and the sordid suit began.

I realize, of course, Adrian, that you had nothing to do with the conduct of the trial, that Ernest Saunders had completely replaced you at the heated command of old Mrs. Lounsbury, furious at the visitation rights you had taken it on yourself to offer me. I have little doubt that she believed you had been seduced by the wily maneuvers of her slut of a daughter-in-law, and had probably only been persuaded by Mr. Saunders not to subpoena you as a reluctant witness to the depravity of my character.

Certainly your partner was a lawyer after her own heart. He conducted the case himself with the cold grim passion of a Spanish grand inquisitor exposing the wicked doctrines of a heretic. His cool satirical examination of the witnesses, including my own mother, who had been somehow induced to betray me, only partially veiled his satisfaction at watching his victim writhe in the flames. How attorneys for the rich and established love it when the aura of moral righteousness allows them to unchain the sadism that they are usually at such pains to hide from the public eye! Most of the time they have to appear open-minded, free of prejudice, uncontaminated by violent emotion, so what a relief it must be when a clear case of immorality permits them to pound a defendant to bits! I think I am one of the few souls who have seen the legendary Ernest Saunders as his real self. He was far more interested in bringing me down than in obtaining a settlement less injurious to the boys.

His most dramatic moment came when he apologized to the jury for having to expose them to a case of perversion and requested the judge to clear the courtroom before introducing evidence of my relations with Sophie Laplace. How that jury licked its lips!

It was greatly to its credit, however, that in granting my mother-in-law the requested custody of my sons they increased my visitation rights and rendered them independent of old Mrs. Lounsbury's discretion. Had Mr. Saunders gone too far and roused some pity for me? Or had there been a secret philanderer or a closet lesbian on that jury?

I do not know how I should have survived the case had you not, in open defiance of your partner, come to my aid. It was you who persuaded that fashion magazine that a scandalous trial might actually enhance the interest of its subscribers in a new editor long familiar to readers of the society pages. I was able to make a success of my job and recapture some of the affection of my boys. When their grandmother died, and Betty Shallcross got custody of them, she let them live with me. In my eventual old age I am sure they will look after me. And I owe all that to you.

10

KATE WAS INCLINED to think that our two children had not gained much from their being constantly associated with my law firm.

"The trouble is, Adrian," she told me, "that the name Adrian Suydam has become synonymous with Saunders & Suydam. Bobbie in particular seems to feel he can never get away from it."

I had reluctantly to admit that she had a point. Bobbie had always been a kind of square youth: square in his handsome but unexpressive face, stocky in his strong but shortish build, firm in his few convictions, a loyal and devoted son, but hardly what we call imaginative or innovative in his thinking. People tended to love this honest young man, and his father was no exception to that rule. When he reads this, I hope he takes it as basically a compliment.

He had given his mother and me little trouble in his growing up. His grades in school, college, and law school were good if not spectacular; he was a fine athlete and popular with his classmates. He married young, in his first year at Harvard Law, and wholly appropriately. Janet was a Bobbie of her own sex: blond, athletic, openly cheerful, and seemingly satisfied with herself and her immediate environment. I had rather assumed that, with his respectable but middle-of-the-class marks, Bobbie would apply for a job with firms less exacting than mine, as Ernest would hardly look at a man who wasn't law review, and I was surprised, not only that his first call was to Saunders & Suydam, but that Ernest himself interviewed and employed him.

Kate was frankly upset.

"Did he even tell you he was applying to the firm?" she demanded of me.

"He did not. I think he knew that I thought he didn't have a chance there and wanted to spare me the argument."

"So you didn't discuss where he should apply at all."

"It was all over before I had the chance."

"So now the poor boy will slave his life away for a firm which will never make him a partner!"

"At least he'll have a great legal education. He won't have to stay there."

When Bobbie came to me to discuss the matter, I mildly reproached him for not coming to me earlier.

"I would have told you, dear boy, what I know about other firms."

Bobbie placed his hand on mine. "I know that, Dad. But I was determined to do what I did, and I didn't want to hurt you by not taking your advice. You see, S & S has always been a magic name to me. The symbol of success. The way to be a man. Oh, I knew I was exaggerating, but, still, there it was. Of course, I knew that I didn't have the grades to get in, and that if I did, people would say it was because you had pulled strings, but then when Uncle Ernest came up to lecture at the law school he gave me a new idea. He told the students that a good mind for business was as much an asset in a Wall Street corporate law firm as the sharpest legal ingenuity. That made me think I might have a chance in S & S, after all. And if it doesn't work out, at least I'm rid of an obsession. Don't worry about me, Dad. I'll survive."

"Oh, dear boy, of course you will."

Of course, I had to talk to Ernest about it. I went to his office and asked him bluntly why he had taken over the function of our employment committee to hire my son.

"Leave the boy to me, Addie," he said tersely. "I know what I'm doing."

"But can't you tell a nervous father?"

Ernest's stare seemed to size me up. He knew a great deal about me—who more?—but less about me as a parent. At length he appeared to relax. "I'm trying to find out what area of law he's best qualified in. If he's ever going to be a partner, he's going to have to pull his own weight."

"I didn't suppose he was going to be a partner."

"Then what the hell is he supposed to be doing here?"

"That's exactly what I want to find out."

"Oh, leave your boy to me, Addie," Ernest repeated. "The time comes when fathers should release their iron grip on their cubs."

Well, what else could I do? Bobbie had taken the job. He had always been in awe of Uncle Ernest; now he adored him. And in the next years—for he stuck to the job—I came to see the logic of what Ernest was doing with him. He was shifting him from department to department to see where he best fitted. Ernest perfectly understood that my son did not have quite the brain power expected of an S & S partner, and by placing Bobbie at last in the municipal bond section he had him where the discrepancy would least show. There an excellent memory and a keen nose for error, plus the ability to get on with tedious city politicians, counted for more than the subtlest legal ingenuity. Bobbie came to rest in that department and remained there contentedly for the next five years, gaining a reputation for good and accurate work, while at home his equally contented wife produced three beautiful babies. When the middle-aged partner in charge of the municipals suddenly died, I was startled to realize that Bobbie might be his successor.

I was so excited by this that I didn't dare discuss it with anyone, including Bobbie, whose possibly false hopes I did not want to arouse. But the matter, as it turned out, was thrust upon me in an unexpected fashion.

One of my contributions to the firm was the institution of an annual outing on a spring day when the partners and associates (but no spouses) left the city in rented buses or their own cars to assemble at my Long Island country club for games and dinner. Ernest had approved, though typically not without sarcastically echoing Scrooge: "A poor excuse for picking a man's pocket every first day of May." Some of our men played golf and some tennis, others hiked through the countryside, and there was always what I regarded as a repulsive little group that spent the afternoon in the bar. For we had plenty of liquor even in Prohibition, as Ernest was always a violent opponent of the Thirteenth Amendment, which he loudly denounced as unconstitutional, though how a validly added part of the Constitution could be that, he never stooped to explain.

My club was a beautiful white-columned structure overlooking the glorious green of its golf course, with a broad terrace on which we gathered for cocktails before dinner. There were always some associates who overimbibed and talked more freely to the partners than was their usual wont. Ernest protected himself from what he assumed would be complaints by sitting at a table of partners, but I preferred to take advantage of the situation to get to know our clerks better and to find out what their gripes, if any, were. Which is why on that particular May day of the mid-1920s I joined a foursome of laughing litigators who were being regaled by one Tommy Peck, a spry sarcastic redhead with a reputation for scathing wit.

"What's the joke, boys?" I asked, easing myself into the one empty chair at the table. I was comfortably aware of my popularity among the associates; I was regarded as "a partner you could talk to."

Tommy replied at once. "I was telling them, Mr. Suydam, of how Mr. Saunders told off the head of a smaller firm to whom he was recommending a passed-over-for-partner associate. Have you heard it?"

"No, but I'm sure I'm going to."

"When the small-firm man protested that he couldn't

pay an associate what a senior associate at S & S got, Mr. Saunders retorted, 'Associate? But, my dear fellow, in *your* firm he'd have to be a partner!'"

As the foursome burst out laughing I knew they were trying to get my goat, but I decided to go along with them. "I'm afraid that does have a bit of the sound of Mr. Saunders. Even if he thinks that, he should learn not to say it."

But I should have learned that with a group like this one, if you give them a hand they'll take an arm.

"Do you know, sir," my redhead continued, "what the boys are saying about how Mr. Saunders answered a daring partner who proposed that a larger percentage of the firm's profits be distributed to the younger members? He is supposed to have said, 'So long as I get my fifty percent I don't care how you divvy up the rest.'"

This, with the noisy laughter that ensued, was decidedly too much. I thought of a picture I had seen in a nature magazine of a great stag fighting off a pack of wild dogs who had cornered him.

"Mr. Saunders takes nothing like a half of the net!" I told them sharply. "And it's an impertinence to suggest it."

Silence fell at once on the little group. They knew when they had gone too far. "I'm sorry, sir," Tommy Peck expostulated. "I really am. We shouldn't relay the idle gossip that goes around the firm. But there is one rumor that we hear of which you may not be aware, and that we think you should know about. Because it affects Bobbie, whom we all like and admire, as we do you, sir."

I had to be touched by this. And alarmed by the introduction of Bobbie's name. "Tell me, please."

"We've heard that Mr. Reed is planning to urge the executive committee to adopt a no-nepotism rule in the making of partners."

I was shocked but not wholly surprised. Douglas Reed was a great one for bringing up new and unpleasant ideas.

"Of course, I cannot discuss any matter that may come up before the committee," I tersely informed the group. Down the terrace I saw the partners at Ernest's table rise. "And now I think we're going in to dinner."

Like other constantly expanding law firms we had long come to the conclusion that the partnership was too large and unwieldy to administer with the efficiency necessary to so various an enterprise, and Ernest had assembled an executive committee of five senior members who essentially ran the firm. Ernest and I were on it, of course, so the vote of only one of the other three in our favor ensured the continuance of Ernest's control. But there were occasional exceptions to this.

Stover Kent, the large, brooding, usually silent man who managed our litigation department, was so intent on his cases that he took only a fleeting interest in the problems of administration that mainly preoccupied our committee, and was happy to leave them to the other four partners. I suspect he believed that, as the one who appeared almost weekly in court (where his silence ceased), he was the only one of us who was a true lawyer. Ted Wagner, our corporate tycoon, was frequently away on business and missed many of our sessions, which left Douglas Reed as the one thorn in Ernest's side.

Douglas was nothing if not independent. You could

never be sure which side he would take. He was a tall, rangy, graying, easygoing, pipe-smoking man of considerable charm and wit, whose smiling drawl seemed to imply, in the friendliest fashion, that surely his interlocutor had the percipience to see the sense of what he was proposing. "We are all men of good will, are we not?" he seemed to be asking, before coming forward with an idea that he must have known would outrage you.

The committee was scheduled to discuss new partners at its next meeting, which was on the day after the outing, and it was to be a full meeting, as even Stover Kent would hardly miss a session where members of his department would be discussed. I was not surprised, thanks to the warning I had received, when Douglas Reed opened the meeting with the question of whether relatives of partners should be disqualified.

"I understand," he added, with a little bow toward me, "that this may be a delicate matter to discuss here. But we all know that Adrian is a perfect gentleman who can put the firm before any personal interest."

"We can discuss the question, of course," Ernest snapped at him. "But even if such a rule were adopted, it could not apply to any associate presently employed. He would have to have been warned when he was hired."

I saw Bobbie grandfathered, as the term was, but I still knew that if a no-nepotism policy were adopted, it would hurt his present chances. He could be excluded for other reasons.

Douglas went on to cite some firms where sons had notoriously been inferior lawyers to their sires.

Ernest almost angrily opposed him. "There are just as many where the reverse was true. And where would you draw the line? With stepsons? Brothers? Nephews? Cousins? And in what degree?"

"Wouldn't it depend," Mr. Kent growled, "on the degree of affection that existed between the two?"

"Well, there you are!" Ernest exclaimed. "The vice you're seeking to cure isn't a question of blood. It's a question of a partner pushing a pet for reasons other than the good of the firm. Nobody in the emperor Hadrian's court looked for a kinship between him and the beautiful boy Antinous."

Even I joined in the laughter.

"But that's something again," Reed commented.

"You mean it couldn't happen here?" Ernest retorted. "Don't be naive. But anyway it's obvious that we're all thinking of Bobbie Suydam, the only one of our associates now threatened by Douglas's proposed ban. I know how embarrassed poor Adrian is by this discussion, and I propose to put him out of his discomfort by deciding on his son's partnership right now. I take it that none of us will hold his relationship to Adrian against him. There was no talk of nepotism when Bobbie decided to throw in his lot with us. It would be brutal to hit him with it now. He has done first-class work in the small but valuable and profitable department where I placed him, and because he is now the only associate qualified to head it up since Ned Poltrow's premature demise, I suggest that we vote on whether to recommend him to the firm as a junior partner. Today. At this moment. Now!"

Such a recommendation would be almost invariably approved at a full firm meeting. Four members voted for Bobbie, Reed abstaining.

Kate showed little enthusiasm when I told her that night. She did not like to see a second generation of Suydams prospering under the shade of so spreading an oak tree as Ernest. She wanted her son to be somebody on his own. Of course I didn't agree with her. I knew that Bobbie, secure in his little kingdom of municipal bonds, would operate as happily as if his department were an independent law firm. The senior partner would have little reason to interfere with its rather routine administration, and indeed so it worked out in the ensuing years. Bobbie was utterly content in the life that Ernest, and not his parents, had worked out for him.

Why had Ernest taken such pains over my child? It was not like him to deviate from his own rigid rules of selecting only the top grade of lawyers applying for a position in his firm. For a long time I abstained from asking, sensing that he found the topic embarrassing, but at length I did. This is what he replied:

"I've always wanted to do something really important for you, Addie, in view of all you have done for me from the beginning of our friendship. But you always seemed to have everything you wanted or needed. Then I thought what *I* would have wanted, and that would, of course, have been something for my own lost boy. That was my clue. I would do something for your Bobbie. I hope it was the right thing."

I averted my eyes, for I felt a tear. "It was more than the right thing. It was perfect."

Kate was touched when I told her, but less touched than I. "But I can't help noticing," she added, "that even Ernest's good deeds redound to his own profit. Bobbie will be a valuable partner to him, and a passionately loyal one. His loyalty in the long run may count for more to an aging Ernest than the smartest legal ability."

11

I AM FULLY AWARE that in the parlance of Wall Street a partner in our firm is generally referred to simply as a "Saunders" partner, without adding my name to the designation. For that is the thing about such a lawyer that stands out in the public mind: that he was chosen and trained by Ernest Saunders. The term immediately suggests an attorney who is smooth, articulate, highly competent, and super-industrious, and, also, I'm afraid, not untouched by arrogance. My partners have the pride of feeling that they belong to a unique and unbeatable team, and this is rarely productive of modesty. I have occasionally been embarrassed by this and have made a point of mildly reproving any expression of superiority made by the younger men in my hearing.

One interesting aspect of the intense loyalty and esprit de corps that has grown up in our firm is how few of the partners have left us for other positions in government or business. We have not had to add to our name those of men returning from public life, like Winthrop Stimson, or Wilkie Farr, or Dewey Ballantine. There was, however, one notable exception to this, federal judge Francis Leggett, a leading light of the bar. He has, of course, been dealt with in my history of the firm, but I ventured to ask him, as an old friend, to write for me his own account of his tenure in our partnership, and he has taken the time and trouble, despite his busy days on his court at age eighty, to supply me with the following:

Memo from Judge Francis Leggett, U.S. Circuit Court of Appeals for the Second District, to Adrian Suydam, Esq.:

You have asked me, Adrian, to write a little something about my years in Saunders & Suydam, and I have given you a brief summary of the cases on which I worked while in partnership with you, but I thought I might add a private chapter for your personal perusal on the subject of the mighty, the incomparable, the one and only Ernest Saunders—God bless him, or do something else to him. You know that he and I still exchange lunches from time to time, and he has come to dinner with Augusta and myself. As Talleyrand said when asked what were his relations with Lafayette: "After seventy, there are no further enemies, only survivors."

I was made a partner in 1905 and remained such until my appointment to the federal bench in 1912, at age forty-one. But of course my square face and stocky figure had been familiar to the workers at 40 Wall Street for the longer period that started when Ernest, with his eye for top law students, grabbed me as the star of my Columbia class and trained me as his principal assistant. I worshiped him as a lawyer and found him an inspiring leader, but I sometimes wondered, even back then, what was behind his cool detachment from the sorrows and troubles of other men. My wife, Augusta, had strong opinions about this.

"The man's a monster of egotism!" she would exclaim to me. "It's cleverly concealed, that's all. That flattering way he has of implying that you and he are the only smart ones in a crowd of dumbbells may be captivating, but just wait. One day you'll find that he really believes there's only one smart one, and it isn't you."

But Ernest guessed exactly what Augusta thought of him. He could be serenely frank. "Your wife's a bright girl, Frank. She sees what no one else does—that at heart I'm a shit."

If he thought little of his fellow men, he thought even less of the Constitution out of which he made so much of his living. I differed with him there: the document that defined our government was to me a sacred text. But to Ernest it was a soon outdated compromise between two competing plutocracies: the cotton-rich South and the mercantile North.

"I need hardly bother to point out," he told me in one of our discussions, "that your Constitution tolerated slavery for seven decades. All it was really meant to accomplish by our so-called Founding Fathers was to provide a loose band to hold together, against an ever-threatening Europe, thirteen very disparate states, each intent on guarding its essential independence. When it became the wish of the majority of Americans, despite heavy opposition, to forge a nation out of the burgeoning number of states, the Constitution was a roadblock. But to tear it up would have looked bad. The weapon of construction was employed to whip it into shape. The commerce clause did three-quarters of the job. You and I, Frank, and the lawyers for the business and financial leaders of the post–Civil War period, have written the real Constitution. And it's not a bad one."

I was appalled by such presumption. "You think yourself the modern James Madison?"

"It's hardly a boast to be better than Madison. One thing you can always be sure of, my friend, is that the credit for building a nation always goes to the wrong men. Liberals rave about the due process clause, though we've seen it powerless to protect a black man from the Klan. Everything goes down before an organized majority. But the lawyers, of whom I was one, who construed 'person' to include a corporation were able to use due process as a shield for enterprising businesses and improve the economic picture. Oh, I assure you, Frank, that redrawing the Constitution to fit the needs of a developing industrial nation was a greater and more beneficent task than those eighteenth-century elitists had any idea of!"

"You make the original Constitution sound like a box that it's a clever magician's job to get out of."

"Not badly put. And we're the magicians."

"Count me out."

It began to occur to me that Ernest himself was something of a corporation: a man-made thing subject to the laws and morals of its creator. Ernest was interested, I was beginning to see, not in money or anything that money could buy (except rare books and art), but in the panorama of a young and greedy country seeking greatness in the seeming infinity of its natural resources. He had as little malevolence as he had pity. He liked to look at the world, and he thought he saw everything.

"It's astonishing to me," I said with a sigh, "that a man as famous for construing a document should have so little reverence for it."

"Ah, but I revere what I'm making of it!"

For some years anyway I was satisfied with my busy practice. My corporate cases were fascinating, and my income was large. I had confidence in the efforts of Theodore Roosevelt to restrain the big trusts and allowed myself to imagine that he represented the future in American thinking and that time would ultimately bring about a satisfactory relationship between the rough business ways of the new rich and an increasingly skeptical public. In other words, I could play my little legal games and let the nation's future pretty well take care of itself. But in the Taft administration, when government and the trusts seemed to be entering into a too cozy partnership, I began to wonder if the liberal cause might not need everybody's help, including my own. This view was fiercely seconded by Augusta, whose favorite brother was a professor of law at Columbia, well known for his radical theories.

"Isn't it a pity," she asked me, "that a lawyer of your stature and high thinking should go down in history as the spokesman for pirates like Gould and Fisk? Oh, I know you never represented those particular plunderers, but it would take a mother's eye to distinguish them from those you do."

"Really, Augusta, how you go on! What would you have me do? Resign from the firm and go in for Legal Aid? You mightn't like what that would do to our income."

"To hell with our income! We'd make out. And anyway I don't suggest that you leave the firm. I only suggest that you use your considerable influence to broaden the base of your clientele. Why shouldn't Saunders & Suydam become known as a firm that will represent anyone with a cause that can be honestly tried in court?"

"You think we're not that?"

"I know you're not that. Would Saunders, for example, allow you to represent a labor union?"

"I think I could talk him into it."

"Try it!"

Maybe it was a plot between her brother and herself, for the very next week, counsel for a small union seeking to sign up workers in a southern textile plant called on me to discuss a suit the union was having with the plant managers. The case involved a constitutional issue raised by the plant's draconian opposition to workers who wished to join the union and was now on appeal to the Supreme Court. The union wished to have a lawyer to argue the case there who was more expert in constitutional law than any in its counsel's firm, and Augusta's brother, who had taken a great interest in the matter, had suggested me.

I realized from the immediate thickness in my throat that I had always been more of Augusta's way of thinking than I cared to admit, and that if I took this case, I was in for just the sort of row that she anticipated. I told my visitor that I would have to take the matter up with my seniors and would have an answer for him in a couple of days. Then I went to work with the office manager to see if there was any conflict of interest. There was none. I now went to Ernest's office. He listened to me gravely and offered no comment. He simply nodded and said he would think it over.

Ernest never strikes until he is thoroughly prepared. I knew by the utter blandness of his countenance when he entered my office the next morning, closing the door behind him, that I was in for it.

"I'm afraid we can't represent your union, Frank. There's no way it can be fitted into our general picture."

"You have decided, then, to allow our corporate clients to dictate whom we may or may not represent?"

"That is not the way I see it. I deem it essential that they should feel that their general counsel is in basic sympathy with the philosophy which underlies the way they conduct their business. The way they deal with labor unions is under constant dispute these days. Bitter feelings have been aroused on either side. If we represent a union, it is bound to be inferred that we support union goals. Even if that is not the case."

"Then we have ceased to be independent lawyers!" I protested, beginning to be angered by his not being angered. "We are simply the mouthpiece of corporate America."

"'Mouthpiece' is a derogatory term. It seems to imply bad breath. If you insist on labels, how about calling us the heart of corporate America?"

"Has it one? In the long run, Ernest, won't we do better, even financially, if we are known as a firm that will represent anyone who knocks at our door with a case that can honorably be tried?"

"Obviously I interpret what is a conflict of interest

more broadly than you do. To my way of thinking it is a conflict of interest to represent a union when we also represent companies which regard unions, rightly or wrongly, as a grave menace to the way they conduct their business. But to the point. I realize that I'm not going to convince you. Will you agree to give up this new client?"

"Certainly not."

"It will go to a vote, then, in the partnership?"

"If necessary."

"You know, of course, you'll lose. But you will have damaged the firm. Unity has always been our particular strength."

"The unity of a despot."

Ernest only smiled. "Think it over, Frank. I'll call you on Monday."

And he left the room. It was now Friday. I fussed about what to do all weekend. Augusta was for my quitting the firm. She had no patience with dictators and wanted me to stand on principle. She was sure that I would do well enough practicing on my own or in a more liberal partnership. It was probably so. But I loved my work in Saunders & Suydam and was devoted to many of my partners, including you, dear old Adrian, and I hated the idea of abandoning all the fine young men who worked with me. When I called on you Sunday night, and you pointed out that Ernest's position was not different from that of other senior partners of similar firms, I was already half persuaded to give in. And Monday morning when I surrendered to Ernest he took it as casually as if he had defeated me in a game of backgammon.

He always knew just what he was doing and the best way to do it. I suspect that he was quite aware that he had taken a further step, perhaps a decisive one, in obtaining an absolute and unquestioned control of the firm. Somehow the details of our conflict became known to every lawyer in the office, and the fact that the issue had been resolved without visible eruption confirmed the general impression of the senior partner's silent, glacierlike domination.

My disillusionment with the great Ernest came to its final climax when, addressing a partnership lunch and without having warned me of what he was going to say, he announced that another proposed new client of mine, a brilliant and radical periodical, had not met the standards of our committee investigating potential conflicts of interest. It appeared that the president of one of our clients had once lost a libel suit against my magazine. I rose to attack this specious argument and demanded that we take time to consider the matter in fuller detail, but Ernest insisted that the case was urgent and mustn't get into the newspapers and that we should vote at this very lunch.

Not once did he look at me in the discussion that followed, nor did he direct any argument to me personally. I might as well not have been there. He obtained his decision, but several partners voted with me. He did not like this at all, though he was careful not to show it. But I could read it in his eyes. His sacred unanimity had been cracked, and I had cracked it.

I now faced the fact that I was dealing with a man who might stoop to anything to have his own way. In our many discussions of world history, Adrian, you have heard, perhaps ad nauseam, my speculations that the so-called robber barons who took over so much of our nation in the second half of the last century were akin to the barbarians who destroyed the Roman Empire. The old order of the wellborn and the highly educated went down before the rampage of new wealth as the togaed senators before the scourge of Attila. What had Ernest done but smooth the latter's bloody path?

I do not know how long I would have stayed in his firm had I not been rescued by my appointment to the federal bench. Since then considerable strides have been made in harnessing corporate power, and I think I may claim to have played a modest role in the process. My relations with Ernest have improved with my new position; even an attorney of his distinction must get on with a federal judge.

I was to learn, however, from a lawyer who was writing a history of my court, something of which I had had no knowledge and that astounded me — to put it mildly. In his researches he had been allowed to examine some — by no means all — of the files of the famous New York Republican senator who had dominated the committee that offered judicial nominations to the president. The man who had proposed me for the federal bench and pushed it, using all his pull with the state party boss, had been Ernest Saunders. It was pretty clear from what I deduced from my historian that without Ernest's intervention, I might never have attained the position that was the dream of my life. But should I thank him?

I decided to ask him just this question at a lunch to which I invited him after the first case in which he appeared before me was over.

"Tell me, Ernest, do you think you were really exercising your duty as a good citizen when you entered the fray of judicial nominations in order to rid yourself of a partner you believed to be out of sympathy with the goals of your firm?"

Ernest paused, as if to weigh the exact significance of the mildness of my tone and the small smile on my lips.

"I wondered when you'd dig that out. It all goes to show, my dear Frank, how quick people are to attribute a low motive to a high act. I have helped to place a legal genius on an important court, and without claiming the gratitude of a single soul! If that is not good citizenship, what is?"

"But you did it for what you thought was a material advantage to your firm!"

"And was it not? Not the least of our glories will be to have been the training ground for a great constitutional lawyer. Who knows? If you play your cards right, you may end up on the Supreme Court!"

It was hard to have the last word in any dispute with Ernest. Yet I tried. "Didn't you safeguard your clients from the liberality of my constitutional principles—which were of course well known to you—by the fact that I might have to recuse myself in any case before me in which they appeared?"

"Even if that were so, which is not at all sure, it would affect only a tiny number of the litigations in your court." I gave it up. Why should I wish to prevent Ernest from having his cake and eating it? Maybe he *was* a good citizen—in fact, anyway.

12

MY PERSONAL HISTORY, in this chapter, is closely
connected with that of the firm. My daughter,
Hopeton Suydam, insofar as she owes any of the many
phases of her intense and highly emotional life to her critical but always loving father, might not be considered one of
my successes. Certainly my wife never thought so. Kate, in
my opinion, was always inclined to be a bit hard on Hopeton, but I can never be entirely sure she wasn't right. Hopeton from the beginning was one of those enchanting, lovely,
bright-eyed blondes, full of a breathless wonder at a wonderful world, who seem designed to be the particular dar-
lings of fond fathers—particularly as those father age. Such
girls get everything they want, it is true, but then, they seem
so richly to deserve it. Bobbie was inclined to resent her, but
brothers do. Perhaps one should listen to brothers—where
sex is absent, observation can be keen. Anyway, Hopeton
was one of the brightest girls in her class at the Brearley
School; she made friends with everyone and wrote scads of
romantic verse. In her coming-out party she was one of the
belles of the season. What more could one ask? Nothing, I
for a long time thought.

Ted Beach was her first big hurdle. He was a handsome dark-haired young man, of obscure but respectable parentage and small means, a customers' man at a brokerage house, who lived, shot, and hunted with social types far richer than himself, from whom he borrowed money that he couldn't repay. He was amiable, predictable, uninteresting, and devoid of ambition. I believe that the only strong emotion of which he was capable was his love for Hopeton; I do not really think he was after her money, though he would have been glad enough to get it. He was a totally ineligible son-in-law.

Hopeton knew that. She was quite sharp enough to see him just as he was, yet she adored him. "I know it's odd of me," she would admit frankly to her distressed and objecting father, "but there it is: I must have him." We were saved only by my happy discovery, through a detective employed by Ernest, and offered by him to me, that Beach had impregnated a working girl, which was enough in those days to convince even Hopeton that marriage was out of the question. For a time, however, she was very violent, and when she finally gave up she hurled Beach out of her life as she hurled the big diamond he had given her (but not paid for) in the East River.

She then went through a period of acute depression during which she would pour out to me her conviction that she was doomed to waste her life. Her mother was inclined to make short shrift of this and tell her to "pull up her socks," but I was always a softy.

"What you need, my darling," I would tell her, "is a man who can stand aside from your moods and realize, with patience and kindness, that they are bound to pass. But he must see that you must not act on them. Don't worry. We'll find him."

And indeed we did. Dudley Perkins seemed in every way to fit the bill. He was something of a ramrod of a Bostonian, large and strong and healthy, a Harvard graduate, of course, with a family tree full of Lowells and Saltonstalls, who had already written a scholarly biography of his ancestor John Winthrop and occupied a seat in the Massachusetts legislature. He was also rich. Perfect? It would seem so. He and Hopeton had met through Bobbie, who had been a friend of Dudley's at Groton School. Her attitude toward this new beau appeared to be a combination of intrigue, awe, and something like amusement, and he was soon in love with her in a plain, simple, direct New England way. Maybe she decided that she was not apt to do better, but at any rate they were married after only a brief courtship.

Dudley was not really a snob, as many of my New York friends tended to suppose. He had an absolute conviction that the Brahmin class to which he had been born represented the highest and noblest peak attained by civilization, but he never alluded to this or boasted about it in any way. To him it was simply a fact. He did not look down on other people or condescend to them. He simply accepted what he saw in the universe. There were these people and there were those. He made me think of the first headmaster of St. Paul's School, who in the mid-1860s was reputed to have answered the question of a pupil whether it was all right for an Episcopalian to have Presbyterian friends, with the caveat: "Yes, if you remember that in the afterlife they will occupy a place somewhat beneath you." Except that Dudley was more generous; he probably believed in a less discriminatory heaven. If his manners were a bit stiff, he nonetheless got on with all kinds of people; he was even an astute politician, as his distinguished congressional career later proved.

For some years he seemed to be in adequate control of Hopeton, and two fine children were born to them. But I was made faintly uneasy by his evident assumption that Hopeton had been indissolubly incorporated into his life, class, and soul by the act of wedlock, that she was now a Brahmin herself and could never be otherwise. I confessed my concern about this to my partner Ernest, my constant mentor, who always took a strong interest in my family, and he told me not to worry. He thought very highly of Dudley, who often consulted him on legislative problems.

"You thought he was right for Hopeton, and I agree with you. She's a fine mare that needs a good rider, and she's got one."

I didn't quite like this. Ernest was never an enthusiast of the opposite sex, as came out, years later, when the question of hiring female associates first arose, and he had taken rather sour note of Hopeton's emotionalism in the Beach business. This was to have its effect later.

I seem to be getting away from the history of my law firm, but it will all tie up. I have come at last to Jimmy Eustis, about whom I had an early hunch that he would bring trouble to my life. It was not that I didn't like him. Everybody in the firm liked Jimmy—even Ernest, at first. He was a small, sharp-eyed, tense, and feverishly active young man, with thick, prematurely gray hair and a pointed countenance that seemed to thrust itself through any barrier it encountered. Yet despite his acerbic wit and an ability always to catch you at your weakest, he had charm and amiability. He came from Utica, New York, of a minor commercial background and had been a star student at Hamilton College and Columbia Law. He had married his childhood sweetheart, June, a passive, affable creature in no way up to him. So far as I could make out, it was the only tactical mistake of his life.

He had attached himself early to Ernest. Indeed, he had waited a year after being once turned down by our firm, hoping for another chance rather than taking a different job. He seemed to feel—and with an odd passion—that he was fated to complement Ernest's abilities, that he would bring to the array of the latter's forensic skills a slightly more inventive imagination, a greater daring in transcending boundaries, less reluctance to shatter precedents. On one occasion, acting with Ernest, he won a famous case by pushing his senior into arguing a constitutional proposition in which Ernest did not actually believe. This was unprecedented.

But it brought about the first really serious discussion that Ernest and I had about Jimmy's prospects in the firm. We had made him a partner when he was only twenty-nine, and I had had no reason to suspect that Ernest had any real reservations on the subject. But he had. And now the essential difference between the law firm that Ernest had envisioned and the usual run of big firms began to emerge. I had always known about it, of course, but in the early years we had looked like everyone else. It was Jimmy who gave rise to

Ernest's finally announcing his doctrine in black and white. And obviously he had to start with me.

Let me sum it up. The bigger partnerships in New York were beginning to expand, and they did not give much thought to how they did it. They did not hesitate to merge with other firms that had new lines of business, or to take in partners from the outside, sometimes at the expense of associates who had worked for them since law school. It was becoming standard practice to establish branch offices in Washington, Paris, and London, and eventually all over the globe—as Ernest scornfully put it, on every iceberg and mud flat. He took a sharply opposite point of view: he wanted a single, tightly run firm operating in New York alone, whose partners would be without exception chosen from the body of associates who had been with the organization since their graduation from law school, usually high-graded Harvard Law men. The associates not chosen for partner would be urged to seek other jobs, but great care was given to see that they should get good ones, with the result that they frequently did better than the chosen, and remained faithful alumni of our firm. All this helped to create a strong esprit de corps and to make the firm a formidable united legal force.

Ernest complained to me that Jimmy was always casting sheep's eyes at Washington, where he had on different occasions already had considerable success representing taxpayers and even government agencies.

"He's always after me to establish a branch office there," Ernest fumed. "He tells me that if we open one and let him manage it, he'll guarantee that the fees he makes will not only carry the new office, but in time may even rival our New York income!"

"Stranger things have happened," I observed.

"That may be, Addie, but I don't want strange things happening to me. And I don't want my control of the firm yanked out of my hands by the likes of Jimmy Eustis. I suppose you're aware that he's already taken advantage of your 'in' with the president to crawl into the great Theodore's lap."

"I have myself introduced him to the president, Ernest," I retorted with dignity. "And nobody crawls into Theodore's lap. I doubt it would be a very comfortable place to be in."

"Well, at least the big-game hunter couldn't shoot you there. He might hurt himself."

"I know what you think of our president, Ernest, and it will get neither of us anywhere to discuss it. But you can't deny that he has a brain, and if he has found Jimmy useful on occasion, he must have good grounds for it."

"But the way Eustis slithers around the capital, making sweet talk with this political group or that!" Ernest exclaimed in disgust. "Is he going to end up as a sleek lobbyist? I've heard he advises a group of Panamanians who are plotting a revolution against Colombia so they can sell the rights to build a canal to Uncle Sam! Oh, it makes me sick! A decent lawyer sits in his office and lets the client come to him!"

"Have you always done just that, Ernest?"

"At any rate, I've tried."

"Look, Ernest. This is not just a question of Jimmy Eustis and a Washington office. It's a question of the future of the firm. Some of our younger partners are becoming distinctly restive. They don't go to you because they're still in awe of you. They come to me. If you're God, call me the Virgin Mary. I'm supposed to be more flexible. Nobody wants any drastic change in the way you run the firm, but they think you're a bit too rigid about minor changes. I really don't see what harm will be done if we allow Jimmy Eustis to set up a small office in the capital. If it doesn't work out, we can close it right down. What's the big deal? And everyone will see that Ernest Saunders knows how to compromise in some of the details of his overall plan."

Ernest was silent for some moments. At such a time he could be very still indeed. But when he spoke his voice shook a little.

"I never thought you'd be against me, Addie."

"Would I really be your friend if I never was?"

He rose now and seemed prepared to leave my office. But he turned at the door. "You can tell Eustis that he can have his Washington office. But with only one partner in it and two associates."

"You tell him, Ernest. He'll be so pleased."

"I simply can't." And he left me.

Thus our firm came to be represented in the nation's capital. It was an instant success. It never, of course, was more than a mushroom at the feet, so to speak, of the great oak tree of the New York office, but it was a notable mushroom, and even a reluctant Ernest gave way before the ultimate necessity of increasing the partners on the banks of the Potomac from one to three, and the clerks from two to eight.

Kate and I were constant weekend visitors in Washington in those years, not so much for the office there, with which I had little enough to do, but because Hopeton's husband, Dudley Perkins, was now established as a Massachusetts congressman of rising importance and Hopeton herself had become a leading hostess in Georgetown. They had a handsome Greek Revival house and two beautiful grandchildren of mine, and weekends there in the lovely Washington spring had become one of the delights of my life.

But there was not only an apple in that garden; there was a serpent.

Hopeton in the early years of her marriage had seemed quite content with her bargain. If it had involved an element of compromise, after the flurry of the Beach affair, it had nonetheless appeared to be well worth it. Dudley was a good man, a worthy citizen, a loyal spouse. Her social and financial position was all that the biggest snob could have wished. But she was witty and capricious and fun-loving and easily bored. And Dudley was rigidly conventional, highly methodical, and utterly convinced that nothing could go wrong in his life, his family, or his marriage. How could it when a Boston god had arranged things so perfectly?

And how could trouble come from anyone as harmless as the amiable and ever-grinning little Jimmy Eustis? Hopeton had grown up very much as a child of Saunders & Suydam. She had known well all the partners and their families, and as a girl had delighted in the wit of the young Jimmy, only a half-dozen years her senior. When he moved to Washington, it was natural that she should undertake to launch him into the society of the capital in which she already played a prominent role, nor was she in the least put out by the fact that his wife was something of a *malade imaginaire* and always preferred staying home with her children to going out. So long as Jimmy felt free to leave his spouse to her own devices, Hopeton was enchanted to have one of the most brilliant and talked of lawyers in the city as the constant extra man in a house she was trying to turn into a political salon.

Hopeton and Jimmy were an explosively congenial pair. They laughed at the same things and mocked the same things, titillating without ever too much shocking the rather serious Washington of Theodore Roosevelt, tinted as it was with what many saw as the golden air of an incipient American imperialism. Independence and individualism were in the air, if not carried too far, and Hopeton saw in TR's daughter Alice the perfect model to follow, striking strong poses and making bold statements, but never pulling up stakes deemed fundamental. She let Jimmy escort her to parties that Dudley considered not worth his political while, yet no one seemed to question the solidity of her marriage. Certainly Dudley didn't.

My wife was the first person to warn me that Hopeton was carrying things too far. Kate objected to Jimmy's prominence at Hopeton's dinner parties. He was too much consulted by his hostess; he was always on top of the news: he had just been talking to the German ambassador; he had a client who was close to the Sultan of Morocco; he had a tip as to the likeliest next appointment to the Supreme Court. Yet I pointed out to Kate that he never monopolized the conversation; he was a flatteringly intense listener and would actually embellish an argument contrary to his own by adding substance to it. And he always reduced the heat of any disagreements by supplying a humorous anecdote that reassured the company that they were, after all, supposed to be enjoying themselves. The final point that I made to my wife was that Dudley didn't seem in the least to mind, and, after all, whose business was it more than his?

"Dudley thinks he owns her," Kate observed. "He thinks that conjugal wire that he fancies he has tied around her neck need only be given a slight jerk if she ever gets out of hand. But wires can snap. I'm not sure his hasn't already."

One Saturday morning when Kate and I were staying with the Perkinses, Hopeton at breakfast told me that Jimmy wanted me to lunch with him at the Cosmos Club. Dudley did not seem to find it odd that the message should come from his wife, and informed us that he was off to the golf course. It appeared that Hopeton was also expected at the Cosmos Club, for she said to her mother:

"Why don't you stay here and lunch with the children, Ma? Jimmy says he wants to discuss a firm matter with Pa."

"And are you a more relevant party to such a discussion than I?" Kate demanded sharply.

Hopeton tried to make light of it. "Oh, I provide the comic relief. Like the sleepy porter in Macbeth's castle who admits Macduff on the night of the murder."

"So long as you're not plotting one."

Hopeton simply laughed at this and left the table, but Kate was serious. She had never much cared for Jimmy—who, in her opinion, like her daughter, laughed at too many things—and she had no desire to lunch at his club, vastly preferring to be with her adored grandchildren, but she still had this to say to me:

"If she's going to be seen lunching with Jimmy at his club, it may be just as well that you be with them."

"Why so?"

"It stems the talk."

"Is there talk?"

"If there isn't, there soon will be."

"Oh, Kate, can't a married man have a friendship with a married woman without its being gossiped about?"

"No. Not when they're Jimmy and Hopeton, anyway."

"Surely, Kate, you can't think they're having an affair?"

"If a woman doesn't mind looking as if she were having an affair, she might as well have one. To me the difference is negligible. I don't know what Hopeton thinks she's up to, but I'm certainly going to tell her she should give it up."

"I don't wish to be around when you tell her that! How can you be stricter than her husband?"

"Very easily."

At lunch Jimmy unexpectedly delivered a short lecture on how wrong Kipling was in saying of the East and the West that never the twain should meet. On the contrary, he argued, the East was becoming almost indistinguishable from the West. Every big town now looked like Newark. Cultivated Europeans and Asians used to blame the commercialization and vulgarization of the world on America. They were wrong. It wasn't American; it simply started in America — it was modern times. And as Henry James acutely pointed out, the masses the world over loved it!

I knew Jimmy well enough to see that this was only an

introduction to something he wanted to put before me. "What are you leading to, Jimmy?"

"What I'm getting at, Adrian, is that there are forces at work in society that are futile to resist. We may not like the commercialization of everything, but there it is. The big law firms are becoming big business. They are no longer the tight little partnerships of congenial men united in their devotion to the practice of law. They are becoming large organizations with offices all over the world more interested in expanding their practice into every possible field than they are in the devoted study of the common law or drafting the perfect brief."

I didn't pretend to be interested. "What is your proposal, Jimmy?"

He smiled and nodded, recognizing that further delay was futile. He then proceeded to outline to me his plan to merge with an already established Washington firm, with the anticipated result that the District of Columbia branch would constitute at least a third of our total partnership. He contended that the enlarged firm would be in a position to represent foreign governments as well as American corporations, that it would ultimately become a power in the land.

"I assume," I interjected when I at last saw an opening, "that you have taken into consideration the simple little fact that Ernest will oppose your project heart and soul."

"But that's just why I've asked you to come here today," Jimmy responded with enthusiasm. "You're the one person who can make him see the light of day. You have always been the balancing factor in his governance of the firm. You're the one person he'll always listen to."

Here, greatly to my surprise and irritation, Hopeton broke into the discussion. "Oh, Daddy, you must listen to Jimmy! You've always been too dominated by Uncle Ernest. No one ever tells you that, but they know it's true. He hasn't anything as a man or a lawyer that you haven't got, even more. Uncle Ernest may be all very well, but he's living in the past and shouldn't be making all the decisions for younger men."

I looked at Hopeton now with something dangerously close to dislike. That a daughter of mine should so coolly step out of her role as a congressman's wife and take upon herself the noisy advocacy of one of *my* partners was an outrage. As was her trashing of her godfather. "Uncle Ernest did not live in the past in a crisis in *your* life," I reminded her curtly. "Without his help you might have found yourself married to a rather different type than your excellent lord and master."

"Oh, it was just like him to put a detective on the trail of poor Ted Beach!" Hopeton exclaimed, stung, perhaps, that I should have mentioned the subject before Jimmy. "That was his sneaky way of doing everything, I'm sure! And who knows? Maybe the detective made the whole thing up to please him."

I was too shocked by this to go on with it. It appalled me to see that Hopeton was capable of hating the man who had saved her, if that saving had been at the smallest cost to her dignity and pride. Could a woman be so illogical as to seek revenge on a godfather who had cleared the way to her prosperous marriage? As Kate might well say, Hopeton could.

Jimmy saw that the time was not propitious for further discussion of his project. He reached for the briefcase under his chair and extracted a file which he handed to me. "Here is a summary of what I have in mind. Why don't you read it over and talk to me when you're ready."

I shook my head and rejected the file.

"Oh, Daddy, take it!" Hopeton exclaimed.

I resisted at this the urge to snatch the file and rend it in two. "Hopeton, stay out of this!" I snapped at her instead. I turned to Jimmy. "I'm not reading a thing or adding so much as an extra stenographer to the Washington office without first talking to Ernest. Now let us enjoy our food and talk about the Panama Canal."

In New York, the following Monday, Ernest and I lunched at our club as we always did on the first of the week. I had only to mention Jimmy to elicit the following rumble:

"Jimmy Eustis may think me a doddering old dodo, but I'm a lot more up to date on what he's up to than he may think. I have someone in the Washington office who lets me know exactly what goes on there. I am perfectly aware of his utterly unauthorized dealings with the firm of Switzer & Clare and his wild plans for a merger."

"It's not a thing, I take it, that you're willing even to discuss."

"For what do you take me, Addie? Of course not. If he has the gall to bring the matter to a vote at a partners' meeting, not only will he lose, but I shall request his resignation from the firm."

I gasped. "But, Ernie, isn't that going too far? He's a

first-class lawyer, and this whole thing is only an idea he's been playing with."

Ernest now really gave it to me. "He's been out of control for some time now, Addie. And I have to add, however painful it may be to you, that you have been little help. Your daughter has been egging him on disgracefully. What she has against me I don't know, but she's hand in glove with Eustis in trying to destroy the firm I've spent my life building up. You should have taken her in hand. The way she's been going on with Eustis is a scandal!"

We were obviously getting into deep water, and I tried to wade back. "Ernest, aren't you forgetting that Hopeton is my darling child?"

"On the contrary, I'm reminding you of it. Our relationship, Addie, transcends family matters. You and I share a deeper bond in the firm that has been our joint work than anything else in our lives, and we both know it!"

However much his attitude disturbed me, I had to admit that there was something of persuasive appeal in what he said. Had not Kate always believed it? While trying gallantly not to resent it? How could I not see that Ernest stood for bigger things in my life than Hopeton's vanity and egotism? But his next remark was a further test.

"In fact, I've even a bit taken your place as a correcting parent," he continued. "Dudley Perkins came to see me last week to ask my opinion of a bill he is thinking of introducing in the House. We lunched, and I took the occasion to tell him that his wife's association with a certain younger partner of mine was causing talk."

"Ernest!" I exclaimed in indignation. "How could you?"

When he said nothing I asked, with a suddenly genuine curiosity: "How did Dudley take it?"

"Very well. He said that his wife was like Browning's last duchess, that her smiles went everywhere. He believes the smiles were innocent."

"I trust he won't do what the duke did to stop them."

"Oh, no. But he said he would speak to her."

Which indeed he had already done. Hopeton came to see me that night. She was almost hysterical. Dudley had quietly but very firmly insisted that she give up her friendship with Eustis entirely. He did not say that her refusal would mean the end of their marriage. He did not have to. It was implicit in his absolute conviction that there were certain prerogatives that a husband could never abandon. Not many, but there they were. A wife recognized his enunciation of them from a certain tone in his voice, very different from his usual sound. I knew that Hopeton would never be such a fool as to give up her position as Mrs. Perkins. Certainly not for the likes of Jimmy Eustis. That friendship was over. Of course, there would be others.

Ernest had a good deal more trouble settling the score with Eustis than he did with my wayward daughter. Eustis saw in the break with Hopeton that the senior partner had declared war, and he now actively worked on the younger partners to back him in his plans for the merger. He now no longer tried to persuade me; he was convinced that I was Ernest's slave. He gained a certain number of adherents, and when the matter came to a vote, he lost, but the firm was badly split. Some six partners and a dozen associates resigned with Eustis to join Switzer & Clare, and many observers predicted that Saunders & Suydam would never fully recover from the row. Instead it marked the triumph of Ernest, whose ever-growing firm moved to a first position in New York and never again suffered a serious attack on his basic principles.

13

I WAS FOND OF MOST of my partners and devoted to a few, but there was one about whom my feelings were decidedly mixed. Bill Wright was perhaps the most brilliant of our litigating lawyers, of whom Stover Kent was the chief, and he made the most dashing appearance in court: strikingly handsome and trimly built, with sleek blond hair, flashing blue eyes, and a strong nose and jaw. Aged almost forty at the time he left us, in the mid-1920s, he would have been a good candidate for a future headship of the firm except for the doubts as to his character held by some of our older members, including myself.

Wright, I feared, was slick. I could never be sure when he was telling me the exact truth. But he made a great point of cultivating my friendship—I was never sure why. He was a passionately ambitious man, and he may have thought that I could help him to rise to the top of the firm, but as he was already a son-in-law of the great Ernest, what more could he hope from me? Mary Anne Saunders, it was true, was his third wife, and he her third husband, and they had been married only two years, with the grudging consent of her father, but still Ernest would probably feel he had to support a son-in-law in any partnership vote. I had to fall back on the lame conclusion that Bill Wright simply found my company amusing. Certainly my Kate found him delightful. You might have thought he was just the kind of man who would arouse her strongest suspicion, but Kate, like many of her sex, was capable of curious inconsistencies, even in her fifties, and Wright was a man of great charm and considerable sex appeal.

I think he liked to shock me and to smile when I leapt to the defense of the moral dos and don'ts of a generation older than his own. He had the reputation of being very much a ladies' man, which his appearance and manner certainly bore out, and he enjoyed regaling me with lurid stories of what he had observed in the litigious field of domestic relations. Nor was he above indulging in the sly hint that in some of his tales there might have been a more personal connection than it strictly behooved him to explain. He seemed to delight in opening up to me a lawless and richly sensuous world that I, presumably, in my dry legal life, had never so much as glimpsed.

"There are sweets in life that even such a brilliant man of your wide and varied experience may not have tasted, Addie," he would explain, using an intimate version of my Christian name that I had never allowed him. But he always got away with it. His impertinences were full of compliments.

I think that one of the reasons that I tolerated the intimacy that he sought with me was that I anticipated trouble in his marital ménage and hoped that I might act as some kind of bridge between him and his aroused father-in-law.

Mary Anne, the pretty younger of Ernest's two daughters, had been a thoughtless, man-crazy, self-indulgent girl who had already made two disastrous marriages from which she had been expensively extricated by her father's firm, the second by Wright himself, to be rewarded by her hand in wedlock. She had learned nothing from experience and was haughtily full of herself, never dreaming that the pleasures of the table had taken off some of the appeal of what had once been a luscious figure and that too many late parties had spread the darkness under her eyes. But she still had enough appeal to satisfy a man as crude as Bill Wright. It was only, however, just enough.

When the fragility of the Wrights' marriage began to appear through reports of Mary Anne's violent scenes of jealousy over her husband's hiring of a pretty secretary or of his spending too many weekends working on the case of a stylish lady client, Ernest, who had discovered that his daughter and Wright had met originally at a dinner party given by Kate and me, reproached me, half seriously, for having asked them together.

"I don't expect my dinner guests to marry each other," I retorted. "And I certainly didn't plan it. Mary Anne had been depressed by her second divorce, and I wanted to give her a party to cheer her up. I've always done what I could for your children as you have for mine. It was she who suggested that the man in our firm who was assigned to her case be invited."

"That should have warned you," Ernest unreasonably insisted. "Mary Anne has always resented what she calls my all-consuming interest in the firm. I suppose she thinks it should have been centered on her. How could it have been? The good lord saw fit to give me two not very interesting daughters. I've given them everything I could, everything they ever asked for. But women are exorbitant. She wanted me as well. Well, she can't have me. Do you suppose that in grabbing one of my partners she's trying to get back at me?"

I was struck by his insight. He must have thought more about his daughters than he let on. "That's not impossible. And look. She's got you upset already."

"What do you really think of Wright? As a man, I mean. We know he's a damn smart lawyer, and I never expected to have to assess him in any other capacity. Is there even a chinaman's chance of his settling down into a faithful husband?"

"I'm afraid I doubt that."

"Couldn't Mary Anne have seen what we see? Or has the perfectly good brain she was born with atrophied in a life wholly devoted to pleasure?"

"Like many women she couldn't believe that the sexiest men are the least faithful. She should have known, because it's true of women, and, saving your reverence, true of her too. Perhaps she believed in the myth that she could make him an exception to the rule. They never can."

"But they're still spitfires when they find that out."

"Plenty of men make the same mistake. They marry babes who anyone can see were never born to be monogamous."

"As Puck says, what fools these mortals be!"

Few people could believe that Ernest could be quite so

detached where a child of his was involved. Some would recall his passionate devotion to his son and question if that could really have used up all his paternal feelings. Even Bill Wright could not fathom the full depth of it, as he confessed to me at lunch at the Downtown Association.

"Do you know, Addie, that Mary Anne and I are hardly ever asked to dinner at her parents? Oh, Christmas and Thanksgiving, but that's about it."

"Ernest has never been much of a family man, Bill. But take my advice. Don't try to change him. No one ever has."

"But the Eric McClasters go there at least once a month, I'm told."

These were Ernest's elder daughter and her husband. Lila Lee had atoned for a bad first marriage with her second to a famous ship designer whom Ernest not only represented but greatly admired.

"Eric's a client, Bill," I pointed out, "and a very important one. He has a great ego and has to be constantly appeased."

"So partners don't rank with clients."

"Partners we take for granted."

"I should have seen from the beginning that Ernest has no heart," Bill mused. "I may have made a mistake there."

"How much of one do you have?" I asked, with a smile to mitigate the harshness of my question. I had long discovered that I could discuss anything about Bill with Bill himself. He was unique, not in his belief that every man lived for himself alone, but in his conviction that every man was aware that he so lived. That men tended to hide this in general conversation was simply to him an example of a widely shared hypocrisy. Thus he would admit candidly to me that he had changed his friends as he mounted the social ladder, just as easily as he would have admitted that he changed his clothes for different occasions, assuming that his interlocutor would have behaved in the same way, even if he chose not to proclaim it.

"Maybe I'd have done better to marry *your* daughter," Bill unexpectedly continued. "But Hopeton wouldn't have me. She was after bigger things. Smart girl."

I hadn't realized that there had ever been a danger of this! I did now recall that he and Hopey had briefly dated and that she had found him crass. Thank God for my genes! But Bill, who lived entirely in the present and in the eagerly anticipated immediate future, had gone on already to tell me about his newest case.

It involved the contested will of one Bayard Tuttleton, the deceased owner of ten percent of the common shares of Texford Oil, which his family had acquired for a song a hundred years ago and tenaciously held on to while it grew into a fortune. Tuttleton had been the joke of the tabloids, a crazy and alcoholic old womanizer who had had six childless marriages. The last wife, Peggy Doran, an ex–Ziegfeld Follies girl, had had the luck to be his widow, but he had attempted to disinherit her, relying on a prenuptial agreement to keep her from claiming her statutory right to half the estate he had willed to his nephews. Bill, of course, was representing her in the savage court battle over the will, which he was thoroughly enjoying.

"But didn't the widow receive a goodly sum of money under the prenuptial agreement?" I asked.

"A couple of million, sure. But nothing like half the estate. And anyway it's all gone. That girl's a real spender."

"And I assume she waived her rights to any part of his estate when she took the two million."

"Of course. That's routine. It left him free to leave her in or out of his will."

"And he chose to leave her out. But I don't suppose the moral question of whether or not she should stand by her given word was even discussed between you."

"Are you kidding? What woman would do that?"

"None of your clients, I take it. On what grounds are you attacking the prenuptial pact?"

"All the usual. That she was a young ignorant girl faced with formidable lawyers and didn't know what she was signing. And that Tuttleton hadn't made a full disclosure of his assets. Painting him as an old satyr and her a naive and innocent virgin. Juries buy that."

"You'd better challenge any woman over thirty on the panel."

"Maybe any over twenty-five," Bill said with a chuckle.

"How did you get to know this lady, anyway?" I wanted to find out. "Waiting with a bouquet of roses at the stage door? Won't she make a rather odd appearance on our roster of clients?"

"Not if she gets the millions I'm seeking for her. They should smooth rougher paths than ours. And no, I'm not a stagedoor Johnny. I met her at a party. Not the kind of party you and Mrs. Suydam attend, I admit, but a good party for all that. Peggy and I got on beautifully from the start."

"And how did Mary Anne get on with her?"

Bill wagged a reproachful finger at me. "It wasn't, Addie, the kind of party you bring a wife to."

He seemed to be inviting me to visit a corner of his experience into which I had no wish to penetrate. I firmly closed the subject by telling him that I had no further interest in his Peggy. It was sufficiently clear now what their relationship was and how he had obtained his retainer.

His case erupted in an explosion of scandalous publicity that dismayed my partners — at least the older ones. Ernest's daily expression became more set and severe; he declined to discuss the matter even with me. Counsel for the Tuttleton estate introduced abominable evidence of the bitter fights and plate-throwing scenes that characterized the decedent's last years with his wife, and managed, despite the objections of the presiding judge, to convey to the jury the idea that the complainant and her handsome counsel had been lovers even in the lifetime of her husband. Bill, on his side, elicited from witnesses appalling evidence of Tuttleton's violent alcoholic rages and fits of seeming insanity. The evening papers made a feast of it all.

In the end the case was settled in what was generally considered a victory for the complainant. Peggy didn't get her coveted half of the estate, but she received a sum that made her a multimillionaire. I was about to breathe a sigh of relief that the wretched business was over when Peggy, flushed with triumph and exultant to the press, made a statement that caused more concern to my firm than the case itself.

It was at a party given to celebrate her new wealth. Reporters were as numerous as the bottles of champagne.

Conspicuous among the guests was her lawyer, whose torso was constantly entwined by the arm of his hostess; equally conspicuous was the absence of his wife. After one of the toasts, the intoxicated Peggy planted a wet kiss on Bill's lips, and when a reporter yelled, "Are you going to marry him?" she yelled back, "Stranger things have happened!"

The next morning I strode into Bill's office and shut the door behind me after telling his secretary curtly that we'd take no calls. Bill looked tired and hung over but, as always, defiant.

"You needn't tell me what you've come about, Addie. I can see it in your eyes."

"And I'm sure you've already seen it in your wife's."

He gave a short laugh. "You heard in the trial about the plate throwing. That must have been where Mary Anne got the idea. She bopped me with one this morning at breakfast." He rubbed a red bump on his forehead.

"Can you blame her?"

"Not really. And it cleared the air. After I picked up the pieces, we were able to discuss an immediate separation."

"Oh, Bill. You needn't go that far."

"Why not, Addie? Do you think our union has been so blissful? And isn't it my duty," he added, grinning, "to make an honest woman out of Peggy?"

"Can that be done?"

Oh, his crude laugh! "Anything can be done with money like what she's getting."

"Don't count those chickens yet. Mary Anne may never divorce you if she thinks she can block your marriage to that woman."

"She's a greedy one, Addie. And you don't know what we might pay her."

"We?"

"Peggy and I. We'll own the world between us."

I was beside myself. "How about the firm, Bill? Have you thought of it?"

"You mean about Ernest? It comes down to that, doesn't it? Will he tolerate an ex-son-in-law in his firm? Is there any law that says he can't?"

"Well, if it were an ordinary divorce on grounds of incompatibility, with no scandal, perhaps no. But under the circumstances!"

"For all your years with Ernest, Addie, you still don't know him. The firm for him comes ahead of anything, even his family, or perhaps I should say, particularly his family. You know the project he's working on now, the great triple merger of three oil companies, of which Texford Oil is one? He will need Peggy's vote now. It may not be indispensable to him, but neither is Mary Anne."

"Ernest can't be bought, Bill."

"That's not the way we'd put it. But let's not beat around the bush. There are plenty of big firms that will want me if Ernest doesn't. I've had offers already."

"I'm sure you have."

"So tell the boss I'm ready to resign if he asks me."

"What about the other partners?"

"Oh, they won't care. Their attitude will be: if one follies girl will make our Bill happy, let him have her. Unless Ernest puts his oar in, which he won't. Besides, Mary Anne has never bothered to make herself exactly popular with the firm."

This, I had to concede, was true enough. Mary Anne had been always too quick to conceal her too easily aroused ennui. I told Bill that I would transmit his offer of resignation to Ernest and left the room.

Ernest had chosen to stay home that day and refused to take any calls. I had to be content with relaying Bill's message to his wife, Bessie. She later called back to tell me that she and Ernest and Mary Anne would come to my office the next day, and that I should have my answer then.

Bessie Saunders had always been something of an enigma to me. She was a tall, slender, very dignified woman, plain in dress and manner, who appeared calmly resolved to maintain the absolute independence that she deemed necessary to the carrying out of her self-imposed duties. Her one known passion was for American arts and crafts, and she benevolently ruled the staff of the little museum that she and Ernest had created to house her ever-growing collection. What her relationship with her husband was it was hard to tell. They never quarreled—at least in public—and treated each other with a rather formal and attractive courtesy, rare in married couples. She was utterly unlike her two daughters and was perhaps the only person whom they held in awe.

In my office Ernest seated himself somewhat apart from the rest of us, on a sofa whose back was against my bookcase. It might have been to distance himself from the disaccord with his views soon to be revealed in his wife and daughter. Bessie sat up straight in the little chair facing my desk, and Mary Anne rather sprawled in an armchair, nervously crossing and recrossing her long legs and smoking. It was she who opened the discussion.

"Mother and I have come to you, Uncle Adrian, in the hope that you will talk Daddy out of his decision to retain in his partnership the man who has dragged my name through the swill of his sordid sex life. We appreciate the fact that your wisdom and great common sense have done so much through the years to keep the firm on an even keel. We cannot believe that you will not persuade my infatuated father to drop his support of this perpetrator of a stinking scandal."

Ernest coughed and sat forward to let us know he was about to speak and did not expect to be interrupted. "Adrian, you and I have often discussed these matters, and you are familiar with my views. But let me restate them. I divide human beings into two groups where the libido is concerned. The first is that very sane minority that keeps the demon sex under a tight and permanent control so that it never interferes with the real business of the moment. The second is the majority who see it as the goal of life, the source of the greatest happiness, who extol it in the arts and mask its viciousness under the name of love. Their trouble is that they rarely find a mate whose feeling for them lasts for the same period as theirs for it. One inevitably tires of the other, but they have never had the wit to learn to cope with this common phenomenon. Hence all the screams, threats, and even murders. You, Mary Anne, have three times in your life discovered that a man was tired of you or you of him. And have you ever tried to face the fact rationally? No. In each case money and precious energy have been thrown to the winds to satisfy a hysterical and pumped-up jealousy. Just because you can't find a man who will break off with you when you want him to, must I lose a first-class litigator?"

Mary Anne addressed herself to me. "Daddy's hopeless, Uncle Adrian. He's never been able to understand that subconsciously he's always hated women."

"Trust a woman to resort to the ad hominem argument," Ernest retorted. "If you'd had one eye open, Mary Anne, you'd have seen that Bill Wright was never going to be a faithful spouse. Indeed, it was for the very dash that gave him that you married him! When I first looked him over, I saw at once what he could do to a judge and jury. Which of us was the better observer?"

Mary Anne almost screamed. "Mummie, I hate to say this in front of you, but do you think Daddy even knows what love is?"

"That does it, Mary Anne." Bessie now rose. "I'm not going to sit here and listen to any more of these grotesque speculations. Will you two please wait outside while I have a word with Adrian?"

After they had left, surprisingly without protest, giving me a glimpse of who directed the family, Bessie, still standing, addressed me.

"Of course, I see my husband's point, Adrian. Ordinarily, there would be no reason for Bill Wright's personal life to cost him his partnership, and I readily concede that Mary Anne has made a mess of her marriages. But when I consider how the poor girl has suffered from Ernest's detachment, and even contempt, I think it's too hard for her to be subject to the insult of her father's continued association with the man who has so mistreated her. Bill Wright will have no difficulty getting an even better position, and are we really going very much to miss so unsavory a character? Tell Ernest to accept his resignation."

"Just like that? He'll laugh at me."

"No, he won't. Tell him that to me it's part of the agreement that has always bound us together."

She left the room with this, and sent her husband back to me. I felt like a headmaster who has just concluded an interview with a boy's mother and was now commissioned to speak to the boy. Was this my formidable partner?

He listened quietly while I did the talking.

"She thinks I owe that to Mary Anne, does she?" was his first comment.

"That seems to be it."

"She's always thought I haven't been fair to the girl. But there's a nasty side to my younger daughter."

My silence may have conveyed my agreement.

"And now," he went on, "Mary Anne wants me to give her Bill Wright's severed head without even dancing the seven veils."

I smiled. "Well, Herod gave it to Salome, didn't he?"

"And then his soldiers crushed her with their shields."

"But that was only in the Oscar Wilde version."

Ernest rose now from his chair. "You can tell Bill Wright that his resignation is accepted. He won't care. My spies tell me he's been talking with Wood & Devens for weeks. They'll match even his greed."

When he left I went straight to Wright's office and gave him Ernest's message. He simply laughed.

"He must be sure of his oil merger. Well, the only thing

I'm going to miss in S & S is my talks with you, Addie. You've given me some good laughs."

"You've given me less," I said soberly.

"This is Bessie's doing, isn't it? I wonder what she's got on him."

14

The answer to Bill Wright's question of what Bessie had on her husband was not given me until after Ernest's death.

The last memo in this portfolio was delivered to me after I had finished my official history of the firm and after its author had read the galleys that I had submitted to her. This was Ernest's widow, and she excused the lateness of her supposed submission on the ground that she had never had any intention of its being used in the story of Saunders & Suydam.

"No, Addie," she told me, as she handed me the little packet in my office, "it's for your eyes alone and for any use that you may posthumously have for it. I know that you have always wondered about the true nature of my relationship with Ernest, and I have appreciated the tact and discretion that you have shown in never making any inquiry. It was nobody's business but ours, with the possible exception of one person whose name you can easily guess. Nor have I ever discussed it with anyone but Ernest himself and that person. Not even with the children, though our adored Mark, with his infinite sensitivity, may well have divined it.

But it's all now so far away and long ago that there's no reason why you, as our oldest and most faithful friend, should not share it."

So here it is.

Letter from Bessie Barnes Saunders to Adrian Suydam dated December 4, 1940:

Dear Adrian,

You have known me longer than most people in my life, and I daresay you find me a well-enough-looking woman for one of eighty—not too different from what I was some decades back. I have kept my figure, my teeth, my erect posture, and a certain, I hope anyway, overall dignity of manner. But I can assure you that as a young unmarried woman in Stonington, Connecticut, I was considered something of a frump, nor was this in any way mitigated by my having two lovely and highly flirtatious older sisters. Oh, everyone was very nice to me—Pa always said I was the brains of our little family—my advice in minor matters was constantly sought—but there it was: Bessie Barnes needed a lot of pushing in the small-town marriage market of the 1880s. Who would ever have dreamed that she would ultimately catch the most brilliant husband in all New York?

No one in Stonington, anyway, which was the hometown of a wide family network of Barneses, Babcocks, Denisons, Lees, and Stantons, all of whom maintained their pretty villas on Main Street even though they spent most of the year in brownstones in New York City, where their men more or less prosperously worked. Their largely British colonial ancestry, including many a whaler, kept them strangely united: there was a kind of Stonington esprit de corps which made them feel that the great metropolis which supplied their jobs looked a bit vulgar and flashy against the sober and modest Connecticut cottages that backed on Long Island Sound. To return to Stonington for the summer months was really to come home. Eventually some of the cousins opted for the more fashionable Hamptons, but they were regarded by the old hands as getting too big for their boots. My mother would have considered a visiting Astor or Vanderbilt much honored by being invited for tea on her small columned porch.

My father died in early middle age, before he had accumulated the capital which would have otherwise found its way into his capable hands, and his widow and three daughters were compelled to abandon the brownstone on East Fiftieth Street and spend the whole year in the family homestead in Stonington. My sisters soon married locally but well enough, and I was left alone with Mother, an old cook and chambermaid (in those days even the reduced had that), and the mild diversions of a sewing circle and Sunday School teaching.

Mother, however, was perfectly satisfied with this quiet existence, and saw no reason that I shouldn't be as well. She found it just as fitting in the scheme of things that one daughter should stay with a widowed mother as that the other two should marry and have offspring. One accepted gracefully the role in life that fate had assigned one. Nor was one role necessarily better or happier than another in a properly organized family. Mother did not recognize what is sometimes called "fulfillment" in a woman.

There was, however, one diversion for me, a somewhat sinister one, as it turned out. Peter Babcock, a neighborhood scapegrace, though a member of our grandest family (what to us was grand), had gambled away his inheritance in the wicked city and had had, penniless and debt-ridden, to seek the shelter of the parental home in Stonington, where he had nothing on earth to do but look for trouble. Of course, he found it, not so much for himself as for others. I used to think later that he was not unlike the raffish Henry Crawford in *Mansfield Park* who plans to amuse himself on a dull visit by making Fanny Price fall in love with him. But where Crawford failed, the wretched Peter was only too successful. With me, of course. He had fatally good looks and a kind of disgusting charm, and almost before I knew it I was caught, hook, line, and sinker. And then his good old father saw what he was up to and shipped him off to a cattle ranch in the Badlands, where he was actually killed in a bar by a drunken Indian.

The emotional chaos into which I was now thrown was something I had never experienced before. But all the way through it I knew that I was fighting for my life and was determined to survive. I think it actually helped me to have no one in whom I could confide. Loneliness gave me a kind of savage strength. My mother and sisters had no suspicion that I had suffered anything but a mild shock, and I was spared the humiliation of their jangled sympathy. I made a desperate resolution that I would never again allow myself to be bound to another human being, that I would fight my battles in life alone, and I began to take pride in the rising wall of independence that I was building around my fragile heart. But was it that fragile? I was beginning to think it never had been.

At this point I received an invitation that changed my life, and I had the force and sense to accept it at once. It was an invitation from Cousin Daisy Gilder to spend the winter with her in her Beaux Arts Fifth Avenue mansion. I knew at once that I needed a change and jumped at the chance.

Cousin Daisy, in the funny way of old Stonington, was a first cousin of both my father and my mother, and had made a rich and happy marriage to Harry Gilder, an iron master from Troy, New York, who, like so many of the newly prosperous, had deserted his hometown for the showier splendor of Manhattan. She was a sharp, sensible, down-to-earth, brisk, neat, and kindly old lady, with every-thing about her in spotless order. She had had the vision to perceive the bleakness of my life and the kindness to do something about it, while at the same time intelligently availing herself of the services of a quiet and dependable companion to shop with her, read to her, and help her with her correspondence and occasional entertainments. I saw my few duties and performed them easily; Cousin Daisy and I got on from the beginning.

Mother had thought it a fine idea. "Daisy won't give you an allowance," she observed. "But she'll buy you things when you go shopping with her. She's mad for the stores. And she might leave you a little legacy one day. From Cousin Harry, of course, nothing. That fortune is all for his two sons. Every penny of it. Anyway, my dear, it should be an adventure."

And it was. The vision of New York intrigued me, even as largely seen through the eyes of Cousin Daisy's rather dull and sometimes pompous dinner guests or from her open victoria as we drove through a beautifully green Central Park or up Fifth Avenue, past the rows of Renaissance chateaux. At first, little attention was paid to me, either by Cousin Daisy's friends or staff; I was treated somewhat anonymously, like a governess in a Brontë novel. But there were always some old Stoningtonites among those who came to the house, and they never neglected me. Word gradually got around that young Bessie Barnes was a "smart cookie" and that if you drew her as a partner at a Gilder dinner party you could have a jollier time than was generally expected in that milieu.

When I first found myself seated next to young Ernest Saunders, already much touted by Cousin Harry as his brilliant new counsel, I assumed that my partner must be disappointed to be paired with a semidependent old maid rather than some diamond-studded dowager or beautiful heiress. But it was not so. He wanted to know what books I had been reading, what theaters Cousin Daisy had taken me to, how I passed my days. He actually seemed to care.

"How could all that interest you?" I inquired at last. "It must seem very trivial to one caught up in the great world like yourself."

"The great world, Miss Barnes, is made up of very small things. Your cousin, Mr. Gilder, told me something interesting about you."

"Cousin Harry did? Why, I thought he was barely conscious of my existence."

"Ah, that's part of his charm! He betrays nothing."

"You find Cousin Harry charming? You interest me."

That may sound impertinent, but I did not mean it so. Cousin Harry was much admired by all, including myself, but everyone was aware of his gruff and sometimes rough manner.

"It's a charm reserved for his few intimates. Anyway, what he said of you was that you were a rarity among American girls. Most face a new situation with the query: what's in it for me? Your query is what can I make of it?"

"Well, I'm as grateful to Cousin Harry as I am surprised. But the answer is not much, I'm afraid."

"Well, we'll see about that."

"How shall we go about seeing it?"

Ernest's reply to this was in action rather than in words. He began by showing me a steady and flattering attention. He took me to the opera; he took me to the theater. In those days a *jeune fille a marier* did not usually appear in public places with a young man unchaperoned, but my never quite defined position in Cousin Daisy's household placed me in a different category, and as Cousin Daisy, a great stickler for etiquette, made no objection, nobody else was apt to. Besides, she was intrigued to find out what Ernest, whom her husband so greatly admired, saw in me.

"Don't be in a hurry, dear," she didn't hesitate to warn me. "I'm told he might be a great catch. My husband thinks he's going very far."

"Oh, Cousin Daisy, it isn't like that at all!" I protested.

I was quite sincere. Ernest seemed entirely content to be an intellectual friend. He sent me new books and articles to read; we had what seemed to me profound and stimulating talks. Nor did I ask for anything more. I didn't, Adrian. Really. I was no more in love with Ernest than he was with me; we had a most satisfactory friendship, and that was a great deal in my circumscribed life.

But all this was suddenly and drastically to change. It was on a bench in Central Park, facing the Bethesda Fountain, on a gorgeous Sunday afternoon in spring, that Ernest, very coolly and clearly, set forth his extraordinary proposition.

"I want to say something very serious to you, Bessie, and I ask you to do me the honor of hearing me out to the end before offering any comment. Will you do that?"

"I reserve the right of getting up and walking off if it's something I don't want to hear," I replied with a smile. "But there will be no verbal interruption."

"That's all I ask. And there will be no cause for your walking off." He paused to clear his throat. "I think I have a fairly accurate notion of what I am and of what I can and cannot do. In a court of law I can argue articulately and cogently for any position that I deem it advantageous for my client to take, quite regardless of whether or not it happens to jibe with my personal convictions. I can, without emotional stress of any sort, *become* my client. But in my personal life I find it impossible to affect an emotion that I do not feel. I am not a man much addicted to the extremes of love and hate. My nature is imbued with a certain coolness that I have learned to accept. When I was a child my mother was always complaining that I did not love her. It was perfectly true. I esteemed her; I obeyed her; I even, at times, rather liked her. But that was not enough for her. She came to hate me. This was hard but I was unable to sham what she wanted. Of course, I only suffered from my small supply of love in the family. Friends do not necessarily expect love, and I had friends. But the question I put to myself was how could I marry without either love or the manufactured expression of it. You may ask: why marry at all? But I want to. I want an intelligent woman to share my life, give me children, run my household, make us a respected and even distinguished couple in the great world. Of course, there are desperate women who can be, so to speak, purchased, but that is not at all what I want. I want a real and competent partner who knows and wants exactly what she's getting. I could offer her a very good life. But I could never offer her the moonshine so many women crave."

I almost rose at this, but he quickly added: "I am not implying that you are one of such. The reason I'm telling you all this is that you're such a complete exception. I believe you have the intelligence to see that we might have a wonderful life together, each getting out of our union precisely what he or she needs. It would be a square deal, one of the squarest."

Well, of course it was the crisis of my lifetime, and I did have the sense not to retreat behind the silly notion that my womanhood was being insulted. It was not, really; it was even being complimented.

"What makes you so sure, Ernest, that I don't want to be made up to by a passionate man?"

"Well, do you?"

"I certainly haven't been. And I don't see much likelihood that I will be, in Stonington anyway, looking after my aging ma. And the idea of becoming a great lady in the fashionable world — if that's really what you're looking for — fails to impress me. In Stonington we learned better values. But what does impress me is *you*. Ernest. You yourself. You are a very interesting man."

"No more than you are a very interesting woman. That's the point, isn't it?"

"The point for me is that you see me as interesting? Yes. For no one else has. To the extent, anyway, that you have."

"I hope that means that you will seriously consider my proposition."

"It means that I will not dismiss it out of hand. And now let us talk of other things."

He rose. "Let us go to the Metropolitan Museum. They have some new digs from Egypt."

When, a month later, Ernest and I became engaged, the Gilders made no secret of their approval. "That young man is really going places," Cousin Harry beamed at me. "He'll be a rich man from what he gets from me alone, and I'm the richer from what I get from him." Cousin Daisy insisted that she would give the wedding reception. "You're like me, my dear. A good Stonington girl doesn't need a dot to catch the right man!"

A constant concern in the early years of our marriage was my difficulty in fully understanding my admittedly remarkable spouse. It was not that he failed in any way to live up to the exact terms of our unique bargain. Our houses and gardens, embellished as his fortune grew, were placed largely under my supervision; I was given money for anything I wanted, and my intensifying interest and absorption in the history of American crafts and design was encouraged by large donations that made my collection almost as important as Harry Dupont's in Winterthur. Ernest never quarreled with me, and the rare sexual congress needed to produce three children was tactfully carried out. I had no complaints, nor did I seek any.

But what was my husband seeking in his busy life? Didn't he have to have a purpose in organizing his great law firm into a force that would bind the natural resources of the nation into a prosperous whole? But was it to benefit the masses or the privileged few? Was it a labor of altruism or a giant ego trip? Did a world really exist for him outside the personality of Ernest Saunders? Was he the ultimate solipsist? When I tried to discuss such matters with him, he always managed, though never offensively, to put me off.

"One does one's job in the world, Bessie, as best one can," he would always end. "What else can one do?"

I was beginning to wonder if my questions as to his underlying motives were not like Pandora's opening the forbidden box, and I had decided to give him the benefit at least of a doubt, when you revealed to me, Adrian, with a friendly but cynical smile, what was really behind what I had considered an act on Ernest's part of singular humaneness.

It was over a terrible strike of coal miners in the bitterly cold winter of 1905. The suffering of the miners' families, the bloody clashes with strikebreakers, the chaos of hate, were sufficiently appalling, yet Albert Rutgers, head of the great company involved, sat comfortably aloof in his Palm Beach villa, adamantly refusing the smallest concession. I finally broke my rule of never interfering in Ernest's legal affairs, and one morning at breakfast, which I always arose to share with him, asked him if his blood didn't sometimes boil at the misery involved.

He gave me a rather odd look. "Boil? A curious thing for one's blood to do. Is there some course of action that you think it appropriate for me to take?"

"Well, couldn't you appeal to Mr. Rutgers to make some concession? He has such faith in your advice."

"What makes you say that?"

"His wife told me so. She said you were the only human being who had ever made her husband change his mind."

"And when did I ever do that?"

"Oh, she knew just when. It was when you set up his foundation. He wanted certain scholarships limited to males of white Caucasian birth, and you would have none of it. No one else, she insisted, could have so prevailed on him!"

Ernest seemed to stare at me for a moment, yet it curiously occurred to me that he was not thinking of what I was saying. "Let us go down there," he announced suddenly.

"Down where?"

"To Palm Beach."

Only two days later, sitting after dinner in an ugly Moorish pavilion facing the sea, with the dry, slit-eyed old lizard, Rutgers, and his nervous fidgeting wife, I listened in awe to Ernest, demitasse in hand, calmly lecturing his host.

"You have to consider, Albert, what this strike is doing to your image in the public eye. You are expecting in a year's time to open your great philanthropical project of building public libraries across the nation. You naturally expect your name to be associated with the improvement of literary knowledge in posterity. But the way things are going every book taken out of a library will have, so to speak, a spot of blood on its title page."

Of course it is history that this appeal brought the old pirate around and led directly to the settlement of the strike. My heart went out to Ernest so fully that you, Adrian, could not resist the temptation to set me straight. I don't blame you. You had to chuckle and point out that Ernest had no interest in the workers but knew that a continued strike was about to seriously damage the company and had been seeking a way to bring Rutgers around — which I had unconsciously supplied!

Yet even so Ernest managed to do good! Was that my trouble?

When a woman starts analyzing her man, it's apt to mean that she suspects that she has overvalued him. I had always known, of course, that Ernest's temperament was a cold one, but now I began to wonder if he had any heart at all. But the perverse thing about human beings is that when I discovered that he did indeed have one, it made things worse and not better.

I am speaking, as you will have guessed, Adrian, you who know all, of Ernest's growing obsession with our darling lost son. What is a heart to a selfish woman if it is not for her? I had learned to accept, however ruefully, my husband's essential indifference with respect to our two daughters. The affection of a busy and preoccupied father is not really much missed by two pretty and popular girls, particularly when that father buys them everything they want, with a smile and a shrug. I knew that it was my job to love them properly and supply the needed discipline, and I did so. Perhaps I should have been glad to perceive a glow in the embers of Ernest's heart, and no doubt I would have been had a spark of it been for me. But it was all for Mark, and though we largely agreed in the decisions needed for the boy's upbringing and education, I always felt that Ernest secretly objected to my having any voice in them at all. It was as if, in drawing up what I had supposed was an accurate list of his assets and liabilities for a premarital contract (though we never had one), he had omitted to mention that any male progeny should belong to him.

Our only really open clash was over Mark's boarding school. Ernest was adamant in sending him to Groton, which I felt had too narrow a social basis among its students. Ernest prevailed, and I don't think it really made any difference in Mark's life, for he was born without a snobbish bone in his precious body, but it started a rift between my husband and myself which was not for a couple of years acknowledged by either of us. I was absorbed with my collection and worked closely, as a trustee of the Colonial

Museum, with Emil Longchamps, the curator of its department of arts, crafts, and design. I was much occupied and, on the whole, content.

Yes, I have come now to Emil. I am sure you have been waiting for me to come to Emil, that dear, dapper, little, nationalized Frenchman, the kindest and most sympathetic of his charming race, the genius of the Colonial Museum, who has been my devoted partner in the assembling of my collection. Of course, you are aware that many people have assumed that he was my lover and have wondered why Ernest has never seemed to care. And of course, you have always known there was no truth in this.

Emil has loved me, yes. Truly, faithfully, and silently. He spoke of his feeling only once to me, and I responded simply by taking his hand and kissing it. He has never but at one other moment returned to the subject.

"Bessie," he said gravely that first time, "you are married to a great man with a single flaw. Only one, anyway, that I can see. I know nothing of his law or business. But I do know that he takes you for granted. All I have to say is that if he should ever let you go, I would always be right there to console you."

You may properly ask now to what extent I returned his love.

Certainly not with anything as strong as his. But Emil helped to keep me alive. He made me feel a thorough woman. I had come to depend on his steady devotion and constant encouragement. And although I had no great desire for a fuller union, there were indeed moments when I could fancy that it might be comfortable and pleasant to share one's nights as well as one's days with such a wonderful and gentle friend. But it never came to that.

What did come, in my early forties, was something I had never expected to have to cope with: a severe and sustained depression. My father had had them, periodically, for no apparent reason, and I had always assumed that I had inherited no trace of the blight. But here it was, and, unlike the paternal case, there were ostensible reasons for it. At least possible ones. The Colonial Museum had suffered a disastrous loss of revenue in the sudden bankruptcy of its principal angel, and Emil's department was threatened by cuts that would reduce his salary to a point where he would have to look elsewhere. Ernest's high-handed treatment of a beau of our daughter Lila Lee had caused a serious family rift, and she had thrown his partiality for Mark in his face with what seemed actual hate. But there was something more to my depression than these things.

I had begun to wonder if I had not, in marrying Ernest, deeply misunderstood what I could still have done with my life. Had my aborted affair with the Babcock boy in old Stonington made me give up all hope for love too soon? Why should I have decided so early in life that no passion would ever come to such a frump as I? Should I not have foreseen my own development into the woman I still hardly dared to see myself as? Was it really too late for me to strike out for some of the things that every woman only too naturally wants?

Emil, deeply sensitive to my every mood, was much upset by my depression, and even more so by his inability to pull me out of it. One day, at the little café near the museum where we often cozily lunched, he summoned up the courage to reintroduce the topic we had agreed never to discuss.

"Bessie, dear, I have to talk to you. Things can't go on like this. You should leave Ernest. Now don't look at me that way. You're killing yourself. I've got to tell you that. You've got to find your own life before it's too late. I know it's hard, but you have to face it. Ernest doesn't need you. Your children are old enough to take it in their stride. You needn't ask your husband for a penny, as I'm sure you can make do with what you have. And you don't care about money, anyway. Sell the collection and buy a small palazzo in Venice. I'll follow you there in any capacity you choose. Even your gondolier!"

Oh, my God, was it really too late? My mind reeled with impossible thoughts. All I could tell Emil was that I would give it consideration, and I walked home alone, conscious only of the fact that in my general collapse, my depression seemed to be collapsing too.

The last person whom I wished to consult was my husband, yet it was just with him that my consultation occurred. He always seemed to know what was going to happen before it happened. It was he who brought it up one evening when we were, unusually, alone, sitting in the library after dinner, I with a book, he with his solitaire. Suddenly he looked up.

"What are you reading, my dear?"

I almost had to look at the title. "*Wuthering Heights.*"

"Why, you must have read it a dozen times."

"Yes. So I don't have to concentrate. I'm afraid my mind is wandering tonight."

"It's been wandering for some time, my dear. Why are you so unhappy? Is there anything I can do to help?"

The words were out of my mouth before I could think. "Maybe it would be better if I went off by myself for a while."

"You mean leave me?"

"Well, for a while, anyway."

"Bessie, you're not being straight with me. Do you mean you want a legal separation? Or even a divorce?"

Was that the way he talked to clients? Or was it simply the way he always talked? He certainly seemed stripped of all emotion. "Well, maybe something like that," I muttered in confusion.

"Do you wish to marry Emil? He's not at all right for you."

"My God, Ernest, what are you after? What are you im-plying? Do you think Emil and I are lovers?"

"I do not. Because I know there's not an adulterous bone in your body. And not many in his, I suspect."

"What then are you trying to tell me?"

"I'm trying to be as just and fair to you, Bessie, as you have always been to me. Isn't that what has made a kind of sense of our joint lives? We entered into a plan, mutually agreed upon, for a union that we thought was best suited for our disparate personalities. For a long time it worked. At least it certainly did for me, and I had thought it did for you. Now it appears to be showing strain. Query. Should it be dissolved or repaired? I am of the opinion that it is too late, on your part, to be dissolved with much hope of be-ing followed by a better state. You're getting on, my dear.

A marriage with Emil would be faintly ridiculous, not so much with the public, which never really cares, and which you certainly don't care about, but with yourself."

"Are you so sure of that, Ernest?"

"Are you so sure, yourself?"

"Go on, anyway."

"Let me outline my counteroffer. The first thing that you need is to escape from your recent sense of being trapped in a life that has ceased to satisfy you. I propose to settle on you outright a capital sum that will make you permanently free of the least economic dependence on me. In addition I will give you my promise to set you free of our marriage whenever you ask it. I cannot make this promise legally binding, as it would be against public policy, but you know I never break my word. Thus you will have the permanent assurance that you are not caught in any trap."

"Except an emotional one."

"Ah, but that is your affair, not mine. I also propose to deed to you a commodious brownstone that I own, with the cash needed to convert it into a museum under your management to house your collection, and an endowment which will adequately provide it with a professional staff and a competent director. I shall of course have no objection if that director is Emil. I myself will be happy to serve on your board and supply legal services and even further benefices."

I sat back in my chair, in a state of near collapse. "And what," I gasped, "will there be in all this generosity for you, my dear?"

"The saving of our marriage. Which is very important to me. You and I, Bessie, know the world too well to wax falsely sentimental. I like the order of our household, the smoothness of your domestic arrangements, the picture offered to the world of a united and respectable family, the utter absence, to the public eye anyway, of any jarring discord. Only thus can I pursue my law practice in peace."

"You're not afraid of romantic complications between Emil and myself?"

"I need not go into what my feelings would be in such an eventuality, as it will never occur. Once a woman like you agrees to preserve her marriage, she can be trusted to the end."

Well, Adrian, wasn't he right? Sometimes I have the uneasy feeling that I let him too often be. But there's no denying that the Arts and Crafts Museum has been the pride and joy of my later life and has proved the glory of Emil's. And Ernest and Emil have worked harmoniously together. It was Ernest who bought the wonderful flamingo room for him from Grand Duke Ivan's palace in Moscow. Would I have had a better life had Peter Babcock not been such a cad in the old days in Stonington? I doubt it.

Oh, yes, there have been times when one has yearned for something more, to be cradled in the enveloping arms of Achilles, when one finds oneself looking for some sign of fervent emotion in the most brilliant and successful of spouses, even if it be not directed at oneself. You might think I found it in Ernest's passion for our son, but there it was soiled by jealousy. He was trying to take something to which I was equally entitled.

You may find it odd, Adrian, but I think the time I thought most highly of Ernest was in those last years when he was fighting the New Deal. Oh, he was wrong of course, deeply and woefully wrong; he had simply declared war on the future; he was raging like a toothless old lion, and I knew it, but he cared—at least he *cared!*

As Emily Dickinson asked: "Dare you see a soul at the white heat?" Well, perhaps I did.

15

I N 1930, when I had passed my seventieth birthday, I made my first and last attempt to retire from the firm. A Long Island university, only a twenty-minute drive from the gates of our summer place, had invited me to teach a course in legal ethics in its law school, and the prospect had delighted me. It would also allow me ample time to work on the life that I had long projected of Edgar White, the American chief justice most admired by my hero Holmes. Old age now took on an aspect for me that was actually pleasant.

"Have you taken this up with Ernest?" my skeptical wife inquired.

"Not yet. But he can't really object to this at my age."

"Oh, can't he? He thinks he owns you, right up to the pearly gates. And maybe even after you're through them. Particularly if he doesn't get through himself."

Well, of course, I was bluffing. I dreaded the moment when I would have to tell Ernest my plans. And when I went at last to his office to do so, his utterly unanticipated reaction totally disconcerted me. For he simply refused to discuss the matter with me at all. At my first mention of the word "retire," he threw up his hands and told me to get the hell out of his office, that he was expecting an important call and had to be alone to think. Ignoring my indignant protest, he got up and literally pushed me out the door.

I decided to wait for a more auspicious time, and for two days we didn't even speak. But when we did, it was to take up a matter the gravity of which took instant preference over any question of my retirement. I had not originally planned to write anything about this in these private papers, not even trusting my Bobbie to have the discretion to handle it. But since then I have discussed it with him, and he has promised to guarantee that nobody would be hurt by it, even if he had to burn my account to ensure this. You see, it involves a crime. Or what was technically a crime. No, I mustn't quibble. It was a crime all right. I claimed it was a moral crime, but Ernest insisted there was no such thing.

The episode — or scandal or tragedy, whatever you want to call it — which made me put aside all thought of retiring without Ernest's blessing — was the direct result of the wrongdoing of a member of my family. This was my first cousin, Stuyvesant (Stuyvie) Suydam, only son of my father's older brother, who held himself out, with what seemed to me ludicrous anachronism, to be the "reigning" head of the family. He shared this conceit with his mother, my old aunt Maud, whose calling cards announced her as simply "Mrs. Suydam." But all this was harmless enough. What was more sinister in Stuyvie, as I was about to find out, was that he considered that his social position placed him above the moral law. A Suydam could be judged, yes, but only by another Suydam.

I have to admit that he was an attractive man. Although inclined to plumpness in middle age, he retained the muscular build of his youth, and excelled at squash and court tennis at his beloved Racquet Club, of which he was thrice elected the popular president. Nor had he lost any of his splendid crop of blond hair or of the hearty jovial manner that went far to make him admired by men who loved sports, both actively and passively. He had always wanted to regard me as a worthy companion and a true Suydam, but he could never fathom or appreciate Ernest, though he was glad enough to come to our firm for legal services and receive from me the advantage of a "family rate" in billing.

For all the tidy sum he was supposed to have inherited, he seemed always to be in need of funds. If he had left his money in the charge of competent investment counsel, he might have been a rich man, but the curse of vanity had led him to suppose that he had nothing to fear from adapting himself to the American principle that every man should work, and he had assembled, with some of his mildly endowed but totally unemployed Racquet Club pals, a small brokerage house that up until 1929 had not done badly at all. But the great market crash that followed a mad decade of booming stocks had gravely altered the financial status of Suydam, Jones, Alien & Smith, known jocularly on the Street as Jesus Christ, Tom, Dick & Harry.

My first awareness that he was in trouble came with his failure to pay a series of minor legal bills for routine matters.

When I drew his attention to this at a lunch—we shared a meal every month or so—he became oddly indignant.

"Are you dunning me now, Addie? Must you have your pound of flesh? Can't you give a cousin a little time? I suppose even a partner of the great Ernest Saunders knows what's happening in the stock market? Haven't any suicides hurtled past your windows?"

I have often noted that the aggressively cheerful sportsman type who smilingly condescends to a world of lesser males is possessed of a hidden nastiness that emerges if a challenge is felt. Stuyvie could still beat me at squash but not by much and he respected me as a relative and athlete. I had had little personal experience with his sudden changes of mood.

"I'm not in the least concerned with our bills, Stuyvie," I retorted. "I asked about them only because your cashier is usually so prompt. My concern was as a cousin, not a creditor. How are you faring in these troubled days?"

Stuyvie's shoulders drooped as he shook his head. The change of mood was again sudden. "Oh, Addie, I don't know what's happening to me. Everything seems to be going wrong. I owe this and I owe that, and when I want to sell something to make myself square it turns out to have little or no value."

He rambled on for some time like this, and all I could conclude was that he was in deep trouble. We ended with his agreeing to my sending one of our firm accountants to get a clearer picture from his cashier.

My man, Jim Owen, came to my office two days later with a rather long face. "It's hard getting all the facts from your cousin's people, Mr. Suydam," he told me, "particularly since his so-called firm is not a partnership at all but half a dozen men sharing office space. I limited myself therefore to your cousin's accounts, and I've made as good a list as I could of his assets and liabilities. If the assets list is correct, he might still be solvent, but I doubt it."

"Why so?"

"Because when I checked the securities that should have been in the vault there were some that were missing."

I felt as if a steel bar had been struck across my chest. I don't know why I so instantly knew that something very bad indeed had happened. Had I always secretly suspected a rotten streak in Stuyvie's character? Why? There were many reasons for the securities to be missing. They could have been sent to a transfer agent. They could have been legally pledged. A record should have been kept, but Stuyvie's office was no doubt carelessly kept.

"Let me have the list of the missing securities" was all I told Owens, and after he had gone, I telephoned Stuyvie to summon him to my office.

"But I have a luncheon engagement," he protested.

"No, you don't," I told him in a voice that brought him to my desk in less than an hour. But there were remnants still of his stubborn sense of elder cousin.

"Your father, Addie, was always glad to come to my father's office when a family discussion was in question, but I suppose things have changed. The nonpaying client may deem himself fortunate indeed if he's not sent to the service entrance."

"We are not concerned with a client who pays or does

not pay," I said severely. "From what my accountant has brought me I can see there's little enough chance of any payment of *my* bills. The question is whether your others can be met and if bankruptcy can be avoided."

"Bankruptcy!" he exclaimed in horror. "You mean there's actually a possibility of that?"

"I should say a distinct possibility from what I have here."

"But how could I live?"

"Well, fortunately, there's your wife's money. That should keep you, if you're careful. The law can't touch that."

"Even if it's pledged?"

With a cold heart I turned to the list of pledged securities. "But Minnie put most of the money you gave her in trust for herself and the children. I drew up the document myself to keep it safe from your market operations. With you and our cousin Eliot Suydam as trustees. You're not going to tell me that any of the missing securities came from that trust?"

"Well, wasn't it really my money, Addie? It all came from me, didn't it, and Eliot was very accommodating when I needed some of the stock certificates that I was selling for better investments."

"And you proceeded to pledge them in your own business transactions? And Eliot knew that!"

"I don't say Eliot knew it. But it was all family, wasn't it?"

I got up and walked to the window. I couldn't bear to look at him for several minutes. Was it plain stupidity or megalomania, or a deeper criminal intent? What was bitterly plain to me was my own folly in allowing him to choose such an idiotic cotrustee as Eliot, another stockbroker as dull as himself. Yet I had thought Eliot as at least capable of knowing that only the income of a trust was available to the grantor.

"Do you know you could go to jail for this, Stuyvie?"

Oh, yes, he did! His ashen countenance told me that however broadly he had deemed himself entitled to handle money in trust for others, he knew that his assumptions were not universally held.

"Let me know the worst," I said with a deep sigh, returning to my desk. "If you don't give me the full story, I wash my hands of the whole matter. And then God help you."

We spent a terrible afternoon. Yet I believe that it was worse for me than for my cousin. He did, surprisingly enough, as it turned out, give me the full picture of his disastrous situation, but I think it was because he believed that a family such as ours was bound to save its head at any cost, moral or immoral, and that it behooved the one in trouble to give the helping hand all it needed. It was only another example of his phoney sense of noblesse oblige. But didn't I share it, too? I couldn't bear the idea of my father's nephew indicted.

I calculated by the end of the day that Stuyvie could be bailed out by something less than half a million dollars, and that there was embezzlement only in his wife's trust and in the pension fund for his employees. It was, however, impossible for a man of his unimpressive financial reputation to borrow a penny in 1930. While I would be working on a plan to resuscitate him, it was imperative to shore up the trust which one of Eliot's partners was already asking about, and I advanced him the needed funds from my own account the very next morning.

It was time, after that, indeed high time, that I should consult my partner Ernest. He always seemed to know, when I telephoned him for an appointment instead of going down the corridor to his office, if it was something vital. He rose now to close the door behind him after telling his faithful secretary, Miss Thompson, that we were not to be interrupted.

"I know that look on your face, Addie. Have you robbed a bank?"

"Yes," I replied, taking the seat in front of his desk.

He listened, expressionlessly as was his wont, until I appeared to have finished. Then he came straight to the point.

"The money you have placed in your cousin's trust. Is that irrevocable?"

"You mean, could I get it back? Not without something of a flap. Eliot's already nervous about having given me the securities."

"As indeed he should be! An accounting would cost him his job, if not worse. But now the trust has been made whole, nobody's going to fuss about it. Provided we keep your cousin solvent."

"I can do that, Ernie."

"And I can do it with you. No, don't protest. You and I have always been full partners, in every sense of the word. But of course you realize what we'll be doing?"

"Oh, yes. We'd be hiding the evidence of a crime."

"Which is in itself a crime. One of which a member of Saunders & Suydam has never been and must never be guilty."

"Ernest," I said desperately, "I never planned to have you involved. I've come to you purely and simply to advise *me* how best to handle a problem that is mine and only mine."

"But you and I are inextricably tied. Morally and, if necessary, immorally. There is no way of bailing your wretched cousin out and saving his name and ours from scandal except with hard cash—*our* hard cash. No one else will lend him a penny. Nor could we properly appeal to anyone, let alone a client, without revealing the facts. Fortunately the cost to us is affordable. The job will be to keep it secret. And I think that can be managed."

I was too overwhelmed to speak for a moment. "But, Ernest, it's been your binding life principle that you have never broken a law!"

"I've always liked the old hymn: 'Once to every man and nation comes the moment to decide.' I interpret it liberally. There may come a moment when the moral choice is a lonely one. If we fail to act, a man will be jailed for a decision he hardly believed was wicked, and many creditors will go unpaid while our firm will get a black eye if not worse. And leftist thinkers, who are already looking forward to how this depression can hurt capitalism, will be elated at this example of Wall Street morals. On the other hand, if we act, nobody but we two will know of it; creditors will be paid, and everyone will be happy except your cousin whose further incapacity to embezzle will be guaranteed by his promise to give up business expressed in oral and written admissions of his crime kept permanently in your possession."

"I can't accept this sacrifice, Ernest."

"Your refusal may activate another duty in me, Addie. Turning your cousin over to the DA."

The smile that we exchanged did little to cut into the firmness of his decision. "There are odd ways of being a man, Addie. Please trust me."

Well, I did. I even let him pay half what it cost us, knowing that in our relationship there would always be ways of making it up to him in the future, and there were. His plan was smoothly executed, and we had no trouble with anyone but its principal beneficiary, my cousin Stuyvie, who objected furiously to signing the confessions that Ernest sternly held before him. But at length he did, and my last worry evaporated with his death from a stroke a year later. Needless to say, I could never again seek to resign from Ernest's firm.

16

THE ELECTION OF FDR and the coming of the New Deal brought a grave crisis to the closing years of Ernest's great law career. In the mid-1930s he was in his mid-seventies, and although his mind was as keen as ever and his working hours undiminished, there was a noticeable hardening of his economic and political views. His lifelong faith in the efficacy of great corporate interests to develop and industrialize the virgin territory of America, even at the admitted cost of some pretty ruthless monopolizing practices, had not been moderated by the fact that the task had been largely accomplished. The frontiers were now gone, and many of the new generation failed to see why big business should be exempt from government supervision. Indeed, they saw big business as the cause of the depression itself and looked to their congressmen to police it.

Ernest had no sympathy for such ideas which he felt were dangerously related to the more radical ones of the Soviet Union. The very tycoons whose vanity and bossiness he had scoffed at even while he worked for them were now accorded a more revered position in his estimation.

The economic system of laissez faire of which he himself had been a principal beneficiary had brought on the great days; now it should be counted on to bring them back. Ernest's theory was that the ups and downs of the stock market were parts of a natural cycle. We had only to let it hit bottom, and then it would rise again. What else could it do?

When I pointed out that this was small comfort for those who had lost all at the bottom, he retorted that he needn't pity fools. He himself had reduced his entire portfolio to cash shortly before the 1929 crash.

"America has grown soft," he complained to me. "We're behaving like children who have lost their toys. Haven't we survived depressions again and again? Does no one remember 1893 and 1907? People regard the boom months of 1929 as a norm to which they're entitled, and they were too impatient to get back there to give Hoover the time to do it! Well, now they have this smiling squire from up the Hudson whom they expect to see pull rabbits out of his hat. I'm afraid rabbits are all they're going to get."

"Everyone didn't have your foresight, Ernest, about the market."

"You did."

"I had the sense to follow you, that's all."

"Well, did I have anything others didn't have? Did I have some secret knowledge? Of course not. I simply watched the signs. And I'll tell you something, Addie. This tightening of their belts isn't going to do our people any harm. They've been living too high on the cob. It was time for a chastening."

This last was not like the old Ernest. Formerly he would have exercised his agile mind to discover ways out of the depression rather than leaving it to its own recovery. He would even have relished the tackling of its knotty problems. But now he seemed totally absorbed, not in finding a remedy, but in thwarting the efforts of others to do so. It was his contention that the cure recommended by New Dealers was far worse than the disease. He saw the National Industrial Recovery Act as an extension of presidential power that threatened the very existence of our democracy. And he joined fiercely in the successful attack on the statute in the famous case which repudiated the administration's power to prohibit the interstate shipment of oil in excess of state production quotas. His argument in the Supreme Court, challenging Congress's excessive delegation of power to the White House, was a tremendous occasion. And his victory, he insisted proudly to me, who had accompanied him to Washington, would be one of the high points in the history of our Constitution. But for one of the few times in our long association, I questioned his judgment.

"If the Constitution really bars the government from taking any drastic steps to combat financial depressions," I asked him, "isn't there a danger that the country will scrap it altogether?"

"In that case I'll emigrate. But it won't come to that. The Constitution will endure."

"But only if it's stretched to meet a crisis. It seems to me, Ernest, that you posit only one possible relationship of government to free enterprise: a strict laissez faire. That, of course, was the philosophy of Justice Stephen Field. But other judges have felt otherwise. The Constitution wasn't handed down from Mount Sinai."

"I know; I know," Ernest retorted impatiently. "You're one of those who think the whole document is encapsulated in the commerce clause. That under that Uncle Sam can do anything he damn pleases. But that is scrapping the Constitution—interpreting it out of existence. Well, thank whatever gods there be that there are still a few Ernest Saunderses around to save the day. If it can be saved."

In the next couple of years it began to look as if Ernest's views might actually prevail. The constitutionality of the New Deal legislation was under constant attack, and the supreme tribunal sustained the attackers in case after case with five-to-four decisions. Justices Sutherland, McReynolds, Butler, and Vandevanter, sometimes known as "the four horsemen of the Apocalypse," needed only one more vote to sustain Ernest's vision of the true economy, and they usually got it from one of the other five.

Ernest achieved a national reputation as the stalwart champion of the old ways. If the right wing regarded him as the sacred protector of corporate rights from the depredations of a mindless mob, the liberal press berated him with irate editorials and cartoons depicting him as holding back the stately figure of progress with claws dripping with the blood of laborers and trade unions. Ernest collected the latter with a kind of glee and hung them, framed, in his office.

Could the government provide subsidies for disadvantaged groups? No. Could it fix minimum wages for women? No. Could it regulate hours of work? No. Could it stipulate pensions for railroad workers? No, no, and no. It began to look as if the New Deal was dead in its tracks through that fatal fifth vote which decided so many of the cases.

When the administration at last proposed a bill that would allow the president to add a new judge to the court for every sitting one over the age of seventy, Ernest came into my office, waving the newspaper.

"We've driven the old fox into a corner!" he exclaimed triumphantly. "Now he's turned on us with a snarl and shown himself in his true colors! A court packer. A dictator. L'État c'est Roosevelt! Even a presidential-ass-kissing Congress will have to throw this one out. And then the country will see the Hudson squire for what he is!"

Of course the bill failed to pass, but the fear of God—or whatever there was to fear—had been instilled in the court, and the tendency to kill progressive legislation was reversed. The victory of the right wing had been Pyrrhic. Roosevelt's program became the law of the land.

As, one by one, the old rulings were reversed or modified, Ernest became somberer and moodier. He made no secret of his conviction that the great days of America had passed and that we were emerging into a drab collectivist society.

"The heroic age of the Roman republic is over," he would complain. "Now we are left to the whimsical tyranny of the Caesars. So long as they give us bread and circuses, we cannot complain."

He spent more time now in his Long Island garden and was in frequent conference with my Kate about new planting. He had a notion of ultimately uniting our adjoining estates into a bird sanctuary, of which my wife approved. But he continued to keep a firm hand on the administration of Saunders & Suydam.

The attitude of the partners toward this varied. The younger and more liberal of them suffered some embarrassment over the wide publicity given Ernest as a kind of Old Testament prophet denouncing the evils of the godforsaken New Deal. Some went so far as to suggest that his identifying the firm with the four horsemen of the Apocalypse might alienate from applying for jobs with us the bright Harvard, Yale, and Columbia law-review men who were finding new inspiration in Roosevelt's brain trust: types like Thomas Corcoran and Thurman Arnold. But the majority of our members found a lingering distinction in the public's picture of the grand old lawyer still at his thunderous best and, even in his losing cases in the Supreme Court, winning four angry dissents. Ernest's fame at the bar had some of the anachronistic attraction to lawyers as the British Crown had for tourists.

But there was another problem and one which it became my painful duty to address. There was a growing feeling in the partnership that Ernest, indispensable as he was as the recipient of the blind loyalty of some of the chiefs of our biggest clients, was no longer in sufficiently close touch with the changing conditions of modern law practice to justify his continued control of our administration. Eventually, a group of very serious partners came to my office with the proposition that I persuade Ernest to increase the executive committee from five to ten.

Ernest threw his hands up when I communicated this to him. "How was it, after the fall of the Bastille, that the messenger answered Louis XVI when the king cried: 'But this is a revolt!'"

"He said: 'No, Sire, it's a revolution.'"

"Exactly. And maybe I'd better quit before I lose my head."

"No, Ernest, that's not what they want at all."

"But they want me to stand by quietly while they pick apart, piece by piece, the firm that you and I have created."

"No. While they modernize the firm so that it may carry your name to posterity."

"You think you can get anywhere with flattery, Adrian, and you often can, but not in this case."

"Listen to me, Ernest. If the department heads feel that they are not going to get what they need from the executive committee, they will start to make their own changes in their own departments. Actually, this has already happened. The litigation department is paying the lunch club dues of its associates. That is not true of the others."

"But that is the end of the firm if it spreads!"

"And that is just what I mean."

Ernest retired to his office behind a closed door, but when he emerged it was to accept the enlarged executive committee. But there was a difference between the way he treated this change in his regime from the way he had treated others. Formerly, on the rare occasions when he had bowed to a strongly urged alteration in an administrative matter, he had never afterward alluded to the concession of power. It was as if the difference of opinion had never existed, and the "divine right" of the managing partner never questioned. The precedent, if precedent it was, was lost from sight. But now when the expanded executive committee overrode him on a point, he went along with them but grumbled. He recognized that he was faced with an irreversible trend and that he would gain nothing and lose nothing either by applauding or deriding the new. So why pretend?

Thus when our dress code was altered to allow for "casual Fridays," he simply growled at a firm lunch: "No doubt, we shall reach the point where total nudity is allowed on hot summer days, though how we will sell it to the secretarial staff will be a question."

Nobody minded his gibes. They even laughed with him. The partners knew that an essential battle had been won, and that it was vital to keep him from withdrawing his name from the firm.

I had a little trouble with him when we hired our first woman lawyer. The major firms were still far from making women partners, and the hiring of blacks was as yet unheard of, but there seemed no point in not availing ourselves of competent female clerks, particularly in fields where we had female clients, as in domestic relations, real estate, and wills and trusts. Ernest was too intelligent not to see this, but he wondered if women were as yet sufficiently trained. When he was persuaded that there were such, and the firm hired Miss Zelhorn, it was typical of him to get her for his own work. He wanted to study this new phenomenon.

Miss Zelhorn was delighted by her assignment to the great man and worked hard and well, to Ernest's often announced satisfaction. She was a plain little dumpy woman, round-faced and seemingly breathless, whose enthusiasm and devotion to her task made her oddly appealing. It was sad that her first and perhaps only legal mistake should have been made in the presence of a particular foursome: Ernest, myself, Dan Rogers, our senior tax partner, and Mrs. Sylvia Tarrant.

Mrs. Tarrant was the tall, slim, elegant, Dior-dressed, pearled and ultrafashionable, beautiful at sixty, widow of a great advertising magnate, known to all readers of evening journals and style magazines, and adored and respected by the caterers of the charity balls she sponsored. For she was known, too, for her benignity, her charming manners, her humanity. And here she was, sitting up straight in the chair before Ernest's desk, intently reading the document he had handed her, her chinchilla coat draped carelessly over the back of the chair. And reading it she clearly was; she was not the kind of great lady who simply glances at papers presumably correctly drawn by expensive and trusted counsel. She wanted to see for herself.

Now she lowered the document and looked up at the old lawyer. "It seems to me, Ernest, that Article Five—is that it? Yes—does precisely the opposite of what I intended. No doubt I'm reading it wrong. You lawyers do have your own language. I'm sure you can explain it to me."

She handed him the document across the desk, and he read it with his usual speed. Then he shook his head, and smiling wryly, handed the paper to Rogers. "She's one hundred percent right, Dan. A little 'not' has somehow made its escape from the document." He turned back to Mrs. Tarrant. "I don't suppose, Sylvia, that you'd care for a job here as a proofreader. We need one like you."

Well, he was making the best of it, but it was still a pretty bad business, and I saw by Rogers's darkened countenance and in the grim look he cast at poor lobster-red Miss Zelhorn what her future was apt to be in the firm. It seemed so unfair that the blow should have been delivered by one of her own sex. Mrs. Tarrant had all the old female advantages with which to subdue the stronger sex; she could say to this man go, and he goeth, and to that man come and he cometh. Miss Zelhorn had none and had tried to arm herself with a tool that men use, law, and Mrs. Tarrant had beaten her even at that game.

Ernest now suggested that we all—Miss Zelhorn excluded—go to lunch at his club while the paper was being retyped and rechecked. I excused myself, and when the others had left, invited Miss Zelhorn to lunch with me. But she tearfully declined, saying she had to supervise the change of the document.

The story has a happy ending, for Ernest refused to discharge Miss Zelhorn, and she survived to become a beloved fixture in the department of wills, preparing the testamentary provisions of many partners. Ernest was proud of his support of her and boasted to me that she had developed the independence and guts to talk back to him.

"She read me a lecture, Addie, on how to treat my daughters, and, by God, she was right. I had given Mary Anne a larger share of my estate (in trust, of course) than Lila Lee, because Mary Anne is always bust, and Lila Lee is married, as you know, to a rich man. But Miss Zelhorn says no, it's all right to give unevenly in your lifetime when you're here to assess the difference in means, but when you're dead Lila Lee's husband might leave her or lose his shirt, and Mary

Anne might marry a gold bug. So even-steven is the rule for wills. And she's right!"

At the outbreak of war in Europe in 1939 Ernest did not share my strong interventionist views. He believed in helping the Allies, yes, but he thought that America should remain neutral, and was even of the opinion that the best resolution of the conflict might be a draw. We had long and even acrimonious arguments on the subject in which he accused me of still being a Rough Rider at heart.

"Like your hero Teddy," he would conclude, "you're still looking for something to kill."

"And if it's Hitler, I'm satisfied."

But all this changed with the Battle of Britain. With the heroic action of the RAF, he saw the reemergence of the spirit of his adored son, and there was never a word from him after that of anything short of unconditional surrender for our foes.

17

EARLY IN WORLD WAR II, in the spring of 1942, Ernest suffered a major stroke, which we feared would be fatal, as indeed it was to be, though he survived for six months. He was confined to his bedroom in the Long Island house and to the tender care of his wife and nurses, except when his old and faithful butler propelled him in a wheelchair down the alleys of his beloved garden. Because of his impaired mental state his visitors were confined to intimate friends. His mind was clear only part of the time; at others he harbored strange illusions. These latter were delivered with all his old preciseness of articulation, so that his interlocutor was sometimes tempted to take them for gospel truths.

For example, on one of my visits, he spoke of a change he wished to make by a codicil to his will. "I keep a notebook," he instructed me, "in which I jot down the addresses and telephone numbers of useful agencies: theater ticket salesmen, plumbers, electricians, car rentals, liquor stores, and so forth. It's really an indispensable compilation."

"I'm sure it is, Ernest. But what has it to do with your will?"

"I wish to leave it to Harvard."

I knew enough to tell him that I would draft such a codicil, and by the next day he would have forgotten about it. Yet at other times he would react to world news with all his old passion and brilliance. One such time was his indignant response to the Supreme Court's unanimous affirmance of our government's confining thousands of United States citizens of Japanese origin to concentration camps without even an allegation of unpatriotic activity.

"They call themselves judges! Men who give in to a West Coast phobia based on nothing but racial prejudice? Who tore to pieces the Constitution it is their one duty to preserve? The Constitution! They wouldn't have even had to cite it had they done the right thing! They could have shot down this shameful despotism on the simple grounds that this is the United States of America!"

Poor Ernest was cruelly mortified by the physical symptoms of his deteriorating condition, such as gaseous emissions and uncontrollable urination, and would admit fewer and fewer visitors until the list was pretty well restricted to his family, his old secretary, and myself. With me, fortunately, he seemed almost totally relaxed.

"There's very little you don't know about me, Addie," he said with a wry smile, after one of these incidents rapidly remedied by his nurse. "And there's a kind of appropriateness in your being here at the end of the story. I'm even sorry I shall miss the end of yours. But something tells me it won't be like mine. You've had a good clean life, and you'll have a good clean end. You may even hit the century mark!"

"God forbid!"

"Why say that? Life can be fine so long as you have your health. We're going to win this war, and 1958, your centennial, may be a good year. But I don't believe the kind of law firm you and I have built together will survive. Oh, I don't mean it won't exist, but in a somewhat different form. The big firms are getting bigger all the time, and I don't know where that will stop. But after a certain point it won't be possible for them to have the homogeneity, the esprit de corps, the intimacy that we've had. They'll be more like big corporations."

At this he paused so long with his eyes closed, I thought he might have gone to sleep, until his hand reached for mine.

"I want to tell you something, Addie, because you've been closer to me than anyone else. Some people think, I'm sure, that I've missed the best thing in life — the thing they call love. They think of me as cool and unfeeling. And it's true that I've largely avoided the tumults of human passion, and confined myself, quite contentedly, to the serene pastures of moderation and common sense. But I did have one passion, as you will well remember. It was for my son. And it was not a happy thing. I always knew that his wonderful generosity and kindness with me were motivated by respect and his profound sense of duty. He never reciprocated my strong feelings. Had he not been my son I doubt that he would have even much liked me."

I had to protest; my heart was wrenched. "Oh, Ernest, that is not true! That is really not true!"

"Well, I may exaggerate a bit. But don't contradict a dying man. Just listen. I was tortured by the sense that I could never be to him anything like what he was to me. And when he died in France, it almost killed me. No, Addie, if that was passion, if that was love, I'd have been better off without it. My relationship with you has been far more satisfying. It has been as near perfection as any human relationship can be. We have complemented each other in the joint task of creating a great law firm, and that is all I have ever asked of life. Oh, I have had my failures, of course. I have not been a very good father to Goneril and Regan." Here he paused to let me join in his mild chuckle and squeezed my hand. "Or even a very good husband to the ever patient Bessie. But I have done the things I could do best, and a man can't ask for much more than that."

"Ernest . . . ," I began, but emotion choked me.

"Don't say it," he urged me. "You and I understand each other. And always have."

When I left his house that day, I had the feeling that I would not see him again and even hoped this would be so. There would never be a better time for him to go than after this final assessment of his commendable life. Even the repressed note of defiance in his tone, which showed his perennial contempt for the many people who would repudiate his philosophy, seemed an appropriate finale for so determined a fighter. His high opinion of me had to be the principal award of my own efforts in life. I suppose there are those who might think it was the only one. But it's too late for me to consider them.

Two days later Bessie telephoned to tell me it was all over.

"You will miss him, dear Adrian," she ended simply.

"We both will. Always."

"But you more than anyone."